THE STORY OF OUR LIVES - DO DRAGONS REALLY FLY?

BY

IRENE TURNBULL-BANHAM

Published by Irene Turnbull-Banham.

Title: The Story of Our Lives - *Do Dragons Really Fly?*
Author: Irene Turnbull-Banham

OVERVIEW

In war, survival is everything, but the heart has a war of its own.

From Londonderry to colonial Hong Kong, a young mother's world shatters when Hong Kong falls to the Japanese Imperial Army. Forced to flee with her children, she escapes under cover of night, navigating fear, hunger and the constant threat of capture.

Across seas and continents, from the Philippines to Australia, she carries nothing but her children and a fragile hope of safety. Along the way, an unexpected encounter with a powerful Chinese Sea Lord leaves a mark that will echo through generations.

Inspired by true events, *The Story of Our Lives- Do Dragons Really Fly?* is a moving tale of courage, sacrifice and the invisible red thread that binds families together, and of the inner dragon, we all possess, rising when life demands our greatest strength.

CONTENTS

PROLOGUE

A family's dynasty, a historical, fictional tale inspired by actual events.

Worthy of note is that the writer believes we are all born equal but different. The difference can be explained as a dragon that exists within each of us, which we can call on at times of real need.

In the shadow of Londonderry's rolling green hills and bustling industrial heartland, a family's legacy unfolds against the contrasting fortunes of pre-World War II Northern Ireland. Londonderry was a place of sharp contrasts: its busy industries, including shirt-making and maritime trade, brought prosperity to a few, while many labourers, particularly women in the factories and rural farmers in the surrounding countryside, struggled to maintain a satisfactory lifestyle.

This backdrop of opportunity and hardship shaped the social fabric of the city, setting the stage for a family story rooted in resilience, ambition and the turbulent years leading up to World War II and beyond. Such a backdrop highlighted the limited opportunities available to young men in pre-war Londonderry, leading many to consider the military as a viable path for those seeking a way out and a sense of purpose.

Through decades of hardship and triumph, the family grows, their lives intertwined with the historic moments that shape the world: the heartbreak of war telegrams, the wistful longing captured in faded postcards from far-off lands, and the stories passed down at family gatherings, rich with both laughter and tears. Each generation brings new challenges and highlights, from the post-war rebuilding of the 1920s to the social upheaval of the 1960s, to evacuations and travel to far-flung countries, and eventually to the globalised, fast-paced world of today.

This is the saga of a family whose memories are preserved in the artefacts they leave behind. These range from a worn postcard sent from a distant shore to a telegram carrying both joy and sorrow. There is also a photograph of a soldier who never came home. And a signed letter of condolence from King George V1.

These fragments of history connect the past to the present, revealing how the choices of one generation ripple through time, shaping those who come after.

The story moves from Londonderry, Northern Ireland, to countries in the Pacific Rim, including Hong Kong (the Pearl of the Orient), Shanghai, Japan, the Philippines, Australia and back home to Northern Ireland, concluding in stone cottage in North Wales.

The story highlights firmly held beliefs shaped over years spent in Asia, where one lives and breathes the fascination that is the Far East. In Chinese belief, we each carry an inner dragon, a powerful and mystical force that remains dormant until it is called upon. The dragon is not a creature of fire and destruction but a positive symbol of strength, resilience and wisdom. Our dragon embodies courage in times of fear, energy when spirits wane and clarity when choices seem clouded. Just as the dragon is revered in Chinese culture as a bringer of good fortune and protection, so our inner dragon reminds us that we possess an unshakable core of power and dignity. When called upon, it rises within us, guiding us through hardship and helping us face life's storms with grace, bravery and determination.

As the story unfolds, the narrative spans more than a century, exploring how love, ambition, resilience and loss bind the family together across the years. Inspired by actual events, this fictionalised tale captures the enduring human spirit, our internal dragon, proving that even as the world changes, the ties that bind a family remain unchanged.

Our main character, Constance-Philomena Briton, feels blessed knowing that she is an integral part of a caring, loving family that needs no words to be spoken to understand when help is needed. Help that will be freely given.

The name Constance means steadfast, resolute and, above all, faithful. Rooted deeply in Greek mythology, it reflects how she is seen by those who know and love her. When she finds herself alone and afraid, Constance calls forth her dragon, which rises and lets out a mighty roar.

CHAPTER ONE

Surrounded by her family, with her trustworthy dragon now resting, Constance felt a rare tranquillity. Her life's journey was nearing its natural end, and she welcomed it with peace. Constance has had a good life, and her Chinese beliefs let her know that her death will likewise be viewed as a good death. Things she was not fortunate enough to embrace in this life, Constance knows will surely come to her in her afterlife.

In a deeply reflective mood, resting comfortably in her East meets West bedroom in North Wales, filled with the most beautiful aroma coming from an exquisite Moon Flower plant, Constance reflects on her incredible journey through life!

But wait a moment, and imagine finding yourself moving nervously along a narrow, dusty, dark and shady lane. The heavy darkness is disturbed only by the gentle breeze rustling through the small trees and bushes that give the dark lane a sense of boundary, heightened mystery and intrigue.

With her hastily gathered personal belongings, Constance has come to the realisation that she needs to leave the relative safety of the derelict, crowded building in which she, her children and several other young families have been housed for the past turbulent month in Hong Kong.

Feeling totally alone, Constance was leading the way on foot to escape a place where only recently they had known such happiness and security, enjoying life as one of the many lucky military families on a tour of duty in the magical Far East, Hong Kong, also known as the Pearl of the Orient.

Under British rule, Hong Kong (Fragrant Harbour) named after the perpetual burning of incense, was gradually changing from being viewed as a sparsely populated group of fishing villages to being increasingly regarded as a centre of international commerce, boasting a fine natural harbour ideal for trading across the South China Seas.

The rocky and precipitous island of Hong Kong is one of 100 islands in the Pearl Harbour estuary. It is not the largest nor the most populated, but the weather system in the region makes it attractive to seafarers. This is due to the weather system of the South China Sea, which from April to October has a reliable south-westerly wind, providing an easy passage for ships coming from the West, while in November to April it provides winds going in the opposite direction.

Believing Hong Kong was safe and easily defensible, with comfortable family accommodation readily available, Constance and her children had agreed to travel to Hong Kong to join her military husband, hoping to enjoy all that the Far East had to offer.

Constance recalls that when she initially read about Hong Kong and why it was under British control, she was intrigued. She learned that, despite sitting on the tip of the Chinese mainland , China had ceded control to Britain. Having lost two wars to the British during the Opium Wars, in 1841 China surprisingly agreed to cede the Island of Hong Kong and the mountainous countryside and outlying islands known as the New Territories to Great Britain on a 99-year lease. This was done to stem the steady flow of illegal opium being smuggled into China from the Indian colonies.

This gave Britain control of both sides of Hong Kong's world-famous harbour, diverting the opium away from China entirely.

Thinking briefly back to her arrival in Hong Kong two years previously, Constance had seen the defence lookout points along the coastal path as she was driven by military transport to join her husband in the army camp, which would, they had anticipated, be home for two to three years. She noticed the heavily fortified coastal path surrounding the entire island of Hong Kong. Travellers were told that in the unlikely event of an invasion it would surely come from the sea. At that time, even though Japan was actively flexing its muscles, there was no talk of war in the Colony of Hong Kong.

Indeed, many believed that the war was unlikely to touch Hong Kong. However, with hindsight, it should not have come as a shock. The Japanese Army had successfully invaded China and Vietnam and was now making its way to the British territories of Malaysia and eventually Burma, so why not Hong Kong?

Constance knew that China was seen as a rich resource to the Japanese, driven by their desire to build a natural resource base of raw materials. It was fast becoming clear that Japan was seeking to become a dominant power in the Far East.

As time passed, Constance began to hear talk of some of the ruthless atrocities that the Japanese were carrying out against their captives. Events were unfolding to indicate that Hong Kong could no longer be considered a safe haven. With little time to plan, the British and Hong Kong Governments decided on the evacuation of women, children and other nonmilitary personnel to places deemed safe at that time. However, British ships were neither readily nor easily available due to the demands of the war effort. As time passed and the invasion became apparent, Constance felt that action was surely needed.

CHAPTER TWO

After much soul-searching and many sleepless nights, Constance decided on her plan of action to flee Hong Kong to a place she hoped would be safe until the end of the war. She shared her plan with other military wives, asking if they would like to accompany her. A small number did. Others were reluctant, believing they would be safer waiting for the Government's evacuation plan to materialise. Deep within, Constance's heart rebelled at the thought of leaving her husband, haunted by fears of what might befall him. But harsh reality prevailed; she had to go. Painful though it was to leave her husband, she went with his full blessing, as he himself felt totally helpless in protecting his wife and children. Constance wept at his abject feeling of hopelessness; they were both totally bereft, but prayed that they would be together again in the future after the end of the war.

Constance sensed the growing unease among the British military. They knew all too well that Hong Kong, by land, stood dangerously exposed. Very few defences were available to halt the invading troops who, with ease, would cross the harbour and ultimately capture Hong Kong in its entirety, together with its highly valued harbour, the gateway to the mighty South China Sea.

Constance's husband had no way of helping, and so here she was in the dark of night, making her way to a small beach on the southern tip of Hong Kong Island. The beach the little group was heading to was known as Repulse Bay, which looked regally out onto the magical, turquoise South China Sea.

Weighed down by thoughts of escape and by the heavy, humid night that hung like a vast black cloth drawing swarms of insects from the darkness, Constance summoned her inner strength, feeling her internal dragon awakening and coming to her assistance.

The small group made its way to the sandy beach, which is usually admired for its magnificent golden sand and postcard-worthy views. Shuffling along in total darkness, the sand, cool between their toes, was somewhat irritating yet welcome. They held tightly to the children, each carrying a precious Chinese cloth bag containing a doll, a toy, a little book or a little car, anything the children thought they would like to take with them to where they knew not.

CHAPTER THREE

Constance took a moment to reflect on how eight years previously she had met and married a British soldier in Londonderry who was offered the posting of a lifetime to a mysterious country off the coast of China, Hong Kong. Believing the time was right, Constance decided to join her husband in Hong Kong.

Constance and her children had bid their family in Londonderry farewell before setting out for the mystical Far East. They were filled with boundless excitement at the prospect of seeing their father again and at the adventure of a ten-thousand-mile sea voyage. It was a daunting task, but one that Constance knew she could do, as the prize was being with her husband. She knew that her dragon would help her no matter what lay ahead.

Only limited information was given to the families bound for Hong Kong. They were told it would be the adventure of a lifetime, little knowing how true those words would prove to be. They had queued for their required inoculations and had been advised to take clothes suitable for a hot climate. However, light clothes viewed as such in the UK were no match for the ninety-nine per cent humidity and tremendous heat of the Far East.

Before setting off on the epic journey, Constance had been guided to take a small white antimalarial tablet. Mosquitoes were known to spread malaria in the Far East. Constance had sought the advice of the British Medical Officer, the army clinician responsible for preparing the women and children for the long voyage ahead. Constance had suffered fits of dizziness coupled with dreadful nightmares when first taking the antimalarial tablet. Whilst told not to give the medicine to the children, she was advised that in time her body would become used to taking the pills, which would continue for the duration of her time in the Far East and for several months after. Constance was told of the importance of rigidly following this plan, knowing that the tablets would not stop her from getting bitten by mosquitoes; they would, however, prevent malaria fever from developing.

As they boarded the ship that would carry them to their father, the children could hardly contain their excitement at the sight of the great vessel waiting in the harbour. To them, it seemed taller than the buildings they had left behind in Northern Ireland. Row upon row of sea-facing windows were uniformly arranged along both sides of the ship. Constance's son immediately took his sketch pad from his bag and began to draw what he called the most magical ship he had ever seen.

The passenger liner was from the Canadian Pacific Railway Empress Group. It was one of the largest, fastest and most luxurious ships travelling the oceans between the United Kingdom, Canada and the Far East. Passengers stood in awe of the forty-two-thousand-five-hundred-ton liner, which promised luxurious surroundings. Entire decks were devoted to sports, and some travellers enjoyed apartments rather than cabins. They were told that the Canadian Pacific Railway Empress Group was noted for setting a new standard of luxury for the Far Eastern route.

Constance became whimsical on hearing that, amongst many of the luxuries said to be on the ship, it also had a vast ballroom, making her heart burst with love, thinking that if only her husband were with her, they could have danced until dawn wrapped in each other's arms. She mused with a little smile on her face.

Her seven-year-old son was totally captivated and fascinated by the sailors and the work they did, tripping and climbing on lifeboats and causing cries of horror as he leaned out over the heaving ship, loving every minute of it. It was this or have him sit forever with his nose in a book, was the thought that often crossed the young mother's mind. It brought a smile to her face when she recalled how, before leaving Londonderry, her grandmother was repeatedly heard to ask, who is the little fella sitting in the corner with his nose in a book. That was her son!

Life on board the forty-five-thousand-ton liner, which was home for some six weeks, had its ups and downs. Rough seas caused many to remain confined to their cabins. Spirits lifted as the mighty ship sailed through calm seas and sunshine. Passengers emerged onto the deck as if waking from hibernation, filling the air with laughter, chatter and a renewed sense of joy.

Members of the crew took time to arrange a series of deck games to keep the children occupied. Whoops of delight rang through the ship, lifting everyone's spirits. The children splashed in the pool, some discovering for the first time the joy of staying afloat. Constance's son was regularly seen walking around the outside of the pool with armbands and a rubber ring and not getting even a little wet. Feet firmly kept on the ground was his idea of time spent at the swimming pool. His younger sister took to the water instantly, playing and shrieking with laughter as she and her playmates enjoyed many hours in the sunshine, gradually turning a beautiful bronze colour.

The ship operated to the system known as seven bells, Constance quickly realised. Seven bells governed the operations on board ship, including meal times, housekeeping and the all-important shift system.

The crew followed these rules strictly, and though the routine felt somewhat restrictive and regimented, there was constant movement and activity that helped the days pass quickly and in good order.

Sailors spent time informing passengers of the route, producing several large maps and showing the children where they were at any one time and what they could expect to see.

Constance asked if they could formalise these short but very important sessions the sailors spent with the children by turning them into real-life geography lessons. This brought more whoops of delight. Children eagerly drew their own maps, complete with diagrams of the things they were seeing.

The children were fascinated to learn that they were approaching the Bay of Biscay, being told that the water was invariably rough when passing through and that the Bay was known for its bad weather, causing many ships to avoid it. One of the children asked why. They were told that the Bay of Biscay is exposed to strong winds, particularly during storms, which can travel far across the Atlantic. The Captain explained that before reaching land, the ocean winds gathered enormous strength, creating vast waves that rolled into the Bay and made the waters perilously rough for ships. The children walked away with some pictures they had drawn of a rough sea, with several making notes of what the sailors had told them.

The second point of keen interest, noted in their little notebooks, was when the liner sailed through the Suez Canal. Constance was sitting with her children when a member of the crew on duty came over to her, suggesting that she move to the starboard (right side) bow as they were about to navigate the artificial man-made sea-level waterway. To everyone's amazement, the canal was almost like a floating bridge. The children were told to hold tight to the side of the ship but reach out a little, as they would nearly be able to touch land with their hands. For the children's benefit, one sailor explained that the canal provided the shortest route from Europe to the Far East, saving both time and money.

Even though it was at times enjoyable, travellers were becoming exhausted from what seemed like a never-ending sea voyage.

Many passengers were left weakened by bouts of seasickness, yet Constance watched with quiet pride, as her son appeared untouched by it. He spent his days on deck, exploring the lifeboats that sat precariously above deck, each designed to safeguard lives should disaster strike.

CHAPTER FOUR

As they neared their destination and entered Hong Kong waters, a fellow passenger called to Constance to look on the starboard side. She looked with wonderment at the fantastic sight before her, including the infamous Star Ferries taking travellers back and forth from the New Territories across the harbour to Hong Kong Island itself.

As she was to learn eventually, the harbour was always chaotically busy, with ferries jostling for position alongside a myriad of smaller Chinese craft, all plying their wares to passengers embarking after long, arduous journeys on the incredibly exciting ocean-going liners. Chinese sampans bobbed precariously on the water's surface as if skating on smooth ice. Standing on each sampan was what, to Constance, appeared to be a wizened little Chinese lady.

Her first impression of Hong Kong and its harbour was one of wonderment. On one side of the harbour were the grassy, steep mountains of the New Territories, whilst on the other side was a wonderful scramble of buildings, all of which appeared to be jostling for position on the overcrowded Hong Kong Island waterfront. Everywhere looked enticing and inviting to her.

After disembarking from the magnificent cruise ship, Constance and her little family were taken by military transport to Stanley Barracks, located on the southern tip of Hong Kong Island, which would be their home for the duration of their stay. They were quickly immersed in the shapes, smells and strange noises that met them, finding the smells at times tantalising and at times repulsive.

By now, most passengers, including Constance, had shed much of their not very cool clothing, travelling light with few personal belongings. Stanley Fort, where they were heading, was a small village at the end of a sandy lane, which followed the coast leading to the Fort itself. This, she thought, would be home for several years. At least that was the plan. The village of Stanley, Constance recalled, was a picturesque coastal town on the south side of Hong Kong Island that was historically a fishing village but had become a popular tourist destination due to its seaside atmosphere, Markets and numerous freshly caught fish restaurants. The town's Chinese name, Chek Chue, reflected its history, while its English name honoured Lord Stanley, the British Secretary of State for the Colonies, commemorating the transfer of Hong Kong to British rule in 1841.

Constance was unaware that as the transport took her to her husband and their future home, they drove along Repulse Bay Road, passing the beach that one day would play a significant role in getting her and her children to safety.

A fantastic view of the murky, grey South China Sea greeted the little family as they travelled along the coastal path. Constance was mesmerised for the second time that morning, the first being when she was at last held in the arms of her wonderful husband.

On arrival at their accommodation, Constance could look out and see the beautiful Chinese junks sailing sedately back and forth. Something inside her seemed to become acutely aware of the beauty and majesty of the junks, wondering whether she would ever get to travel on one or indeed what life held for the people on board. Many, she had been told, lived permanently on board, as they did not have permission to be in Hong Kong and were not permitted to set foot on land.

Thinking back to her time in Londonderry, she remembered often gazing out at the mighty Atlantic, marvelling at the ever-changing panorama, each day offering a view as striking as a postcard. The Atlantic appeared cold and somewhat unfriendly at times to her. Looking out now over the South China Sea, the view seemed full of life, be it with ships of various styles and sizes all going about their business or the people living and working on them. Constance looked out of the window of their accommodation at a mix of little islands, some inhabited and some barren, with only small wildlife living there. She noticed that when the sun shone, the sea turned a beautiful turquoise colour. The turquoise was picture perfect. The view from their married quarter, the name the military used for accommodation when housing military families, was staggeringly beautiful and like nothing she had ever seen before.

Forcing herself away from the magnificent view, Constance began to explore the accommodation allocated to them. The two-storey stone apartment was built to stay warm against the heavy winds and rain of the seasonal typhoons, yet remain cool enough to counter the relentless humid heat. Constance was surprised that the apartment was entered through the kitchen. The first thing that caught her eye was the huge black range, which totally dominated the small kitchen. She had never seen anything like it before and could not help wondering how on earth she was expected to handle such a beast. The other beast in the kitchen was the biggest white pot kitchen sink Constance had ever seen in her life!

An element of relief followed when Constance was shown the Amah's quarters, which she was told would be home for a Chinese female who would be allocated to look after them during their time in Hong Kong.

Constance then showed her excited children the rest of the house, which included a sitting room and two bedrooms, all of which were fitted with ceiling fans and mosquito nets, life-savers for people living in the Far East.

To the delight of the little family, they had been supplied with rattan tables and chairs, built from the hardy, naturally durable material which, Constance was told, would be resistant to decay and insect damage, two things that blighted much of the furniture and furnishings in the hot, humid climate of the Far East.

Constance put her fear of the black cooking range entirely on the back burner when it was further explained that during the time she would spend in Hong Kong with her husband, she would be getting a full-time, living-in Amah. She was advised that a Chinese lady called Hoi Fung was the Amah assigned to them. Hoi Fung was a traditional black and white Amah from the Hakka region, so named for the long white tunic she wore daily over black trousers with evident pride. She knew that the black and white Amahs were highly regarded within the military as the most reliable and well-trained children's nurses and housekeepers in the tropics.

Hoi Fung wore her hair either tightly coiled in a bun on her head or, after her shower, in a long plait down her back. The long plait, which reached past her waist, fascinated the children. Constance learned that traditional Hakka women never cut their hair, primarily due to their cultural and philosophical beliefs. Not understanding why this should be the case, her husband, who by that time had been in Hong Kong for some time, explained that this belief was based on the core principle of Confucianism, which emphasises respect and obedience to one's parents. He added that to the Chinese, hair is viewed as a gift from one's parents and should not be damaged by cutting.

Hoi Fung explained to the children that when they asked about her hair, that her body, including her hair and skin, was a gift from her parents. Constance also told the children that the word Amah in some parts of China translates to grandmother. This helped the children understand Hoi Fung's role in caring for them and the household.

At first, even Constance felt inclined to lend a hand when Hoi Fung seemed busy, but her offers only made Hoi Fung uneasy. It was, after all, her duty to manage the work herself. Constance sought advice from one of the longer-serving wives, who explained that offers of help or, worse still, doing household jobs oneself would be seen by Hoi Fung as a criticism of the quality of her work.

The children found Hoi Fung quite stern and scary at first, as her dialect was somewhat aggressive. Even Constance admitted to herself that initially she, too, had been a little afraid of her and felt the need to tidy the sitting room before bed so that Hoi Fung would not see it messy in the morning. Little did she know that Hoi Fung saw it as her duty to creep into their living area to tidy the room before they got up in the morning.

One morning, Constance heard peals of laughter. When she went to investigate, she was astonished to find both children with cloths tied around their feet, "skating" across the parquet floors. This, she soon discovered, was Hoi Fung's clever way of ensuring that the beautiful wooden floors, so characteristic of homes in the Far East, remained immaculate.

As the word *Amah* (meaning "children's nurse") suggests, Hoi Fung adored the children and cared for them devotedly. She saw this as her foremost duty and the one she loved above all others. Between the children, the laundry (called *dhobi*), and the cooking on the enormous black range, she was constantly busy. She lived with the family around the clock for the whole of their time in Hong Kong.

Hoi Fung seemed "very old" to Constance. She later learned that Hoi Fung had been working for British military families in Hong Kong for thirty years. For the first ten, she had been what was called a "makie learner," which meant she was a trainee. Constance thought this was quite an apprenticeship!

Constance often paused to take in the pungent aromas drifting from the kitchen whenever Hoi Fung cooked for herself. The culprit was a dreadful-smelling fish called *Ikan Bilis*, tiny dried crispy fish bought in large bags from the bustling Chinese fish market. Supermarkets played no part in Hoi Fung's world. To Constance's amazement, she occasionally found her two children sitting cross-legged on the floor of Hoi Fung's little room, happily picking up the smelly fish with their fingers and eating them with great enthusiasm.

"Sic fan, missie," meaning "eat rice with me," Hoi Fung would call to Constance. Constance always declined with polite determination.
"Come on, Mummy, it is delicious. Try some," the children begged.
"Perhaps later," she replied, suddenly finding herself very busy!

The sight of her children cheerfully eating smelly dried fish amused Constance almost as much as watching them being bathed in the huge deep white pot sink normally used for washing clothes and dishes. Mid-afternoon, it was not unusual to hear shrieks of laughter coming from the kitchen as Hoi Fung stripped the children down and placed them in the sink. When recounting the scene to her husband later in the evening, Constance would laugh at how, within minutes, there was more soapy water on Hoi Fung and the kitchen floor than in the vast white pot.

Life in Stanley Barracks was good. The little family was reunited at last, and Constance felt that being part of the military community was like belonging to a privileged club. Strong bonds were formed, and the families supported one another while their menfolk were frequently away, ensuring the security of Hong Kong and its diverse population. Much of their security work involved patrolling the coastal paths and keeping the fortified lookout system fully operational.

CHAPTER FIVE

It was common for the husbands to be away on exercises in the New Territories. When they were, Constance felt responsible for ensuring that the other wives and children stayed safe in the intense heat, especially during the violent typhoons that swept through the Colony with unrelenting wind and rain.

She helped new families stay safe by advising them to remain indoors, staying in the centre of their homes and away from windows, and wait for the all-clear before venturing outside. The military ensured that each household kept a store of two-inch-wide cellotape to crisscross over the windows, which helped prevent the large panes of glass from buckling under winds that could exceed 140 miles per hour during a typhoon.

 Constance learned that many young wives believed they were safe when the eye of the storm arrived, bringing a spell of calm and bright sunlight. She warned them, however, that the stillness was short-lived, as the storm always returned within the hour, stronger than before.

At the time of the first typhoon Constance experienced, she had been told of the danger of being in the eye of the storm. Her husband explained that the storm was surrounded by the eyewall, the most intense part of the system with the strongest winds and heaviest rainfall.

Each floor in the apartment blocks had a shared hallway leading to stairs down to the car park. This space became the place for typhoon parties. Families were required to keep a fully stocked typhoon kit of non-perishable, emergency goods for use when they were confined to their homes, something that happened regularly during the typhoon season. Typhoon parties for young and old soon became fun, with many luxury food items finding their way into the typhoon parcel, including the much-loved Tsingtao and Tiger beers that the military families enjoyed. Those living in each block pooled their resources, creating a veritable feast to lift everyone's spirits. The children found it great fun.

It was quite common for the children to drag their bedcovers into the shared hall, promising they would sleep there for the night only to come creeping back into the shelter and safety of their parents' bedroom when the storm was at its fiercest.

Constance understood the need for these community gatherings. In many ways, they helped her as the wife of an officer, she knew that the younger wives with small children always had someone close by in an emergency if she could not respond quickly. The close living arrangements created natural communities with a strong social conscience.

The Hong Kong government had developed a well-understood system for warning the public of approaching typhoons. Storm Signal One was issued when a typhoon was far out in the South China Sea, giving ships and the general population an early alert. This raised awareness of the danger, although life continued as normal until Signal Three was raised. When that happened, Constance knew that all schools, offices, markets and shops would close within hours. The advice was to stay indoors once safely home.

The next signal jumped straight to Number Eight. Although puzzling at first, everyone understood that the system used specific non-contiguous numbers to allow time to react. At Signal Eight, everything and everyone except emergency services had to be off the streets by law. This meant the typhoon was directly overhead. As the storm reached land, it gradually lost the heat generated by the sea and began to weaken.

There was much to learn about living in Hong Kong, and on a lighter note many of the military wives enjoyed visiting the Chinese street markets for which the Colony was famous. Hong Kong was referred to as a Colony because it was under the rule of a foreign power but not fully integrated, another detail for Constance to absorb!

Constance entertained the younger and newly arrived wives with stories of her favourite market, known as Bird Street. Local Chinese men and women regularly took their beautifully coloured caged birds there to socialise with other birds. Since most people lived in apartments with no access to gardens or trees, this was the only way to help the birds learn to sing. On their first visit to Bird Street, the little birds could be seen listening intently to the chatter around them before opening their tiny beaks and joining in with the most beautiful songs. Owners often shed a tear when hearing their bird sing for the first time.

"To walk along Bird Street was somewhat magical," she told the young wives. "The pretty little birds seemed to come alive, alert to the sound of other birds calling to them, something they would normally hear only when flying free in a garden, in the woods, or in the wonderful mountainous region surrounding the busy and magical city that was Hong Kong."

Hoi Fung, her Chinese Amah, told Constance that she had many cousins, as almost everyone in Hong Kong seemed to, working on market stalls. She explained that this was where Constance could find exquisitely embroidered Chinese lace tablecloths and beautiful ornaments sold at exceptional prices. She also explained that it was considered good manners to barter, assuming one understood what was being offered and expected.

One particular memory surfaced. On her first visit to one of the bustling and colourful markets, her son had noticed a small carved wooden monkey. He asked the price as Hoi Fung had told him. The trader, seeing this was a Gweilo (non-Chinese) little boy who no doubt had money to spend, said "Ten dollars". To Constance's amazement, her son said, "Ten dollars?" thinking this was not much, when the trader replied, "OK, five dollars!" The young boy bought the wooden monkey. He is learning very young, his mother thought, knowing that her son would tell Hoi Fung of his bargain as soon as he got home. Hoi Fung would, Constance knew, feel very proud of him. At times, Constance thought, Hoi Fung seemed to forget the children were not her own.

The most unusual purchase that Constance made was a very tiny white rabbit in an even tinier bamboo cage. Before bringing the rabbit home, Constance, who had taken a short-term job in the city, placed the sweet little white rabbit in her desk drawer to keep it warm and out of sight until it was time to go home. Unfortunately, she had wrapped it in an angora sweater to keep it warm, as the air conditioning was invariably on full blast. However, no doubt feeling bored, the sweet little rabbit ate its way through the jumper, leaving only remnants behind.

Following strange looks from other travellers when carrying the rabbit in its little cage on the Star Ferry heading home, Constance felt somewhat confused, but knowing that the Gweilos, like herself, could fully understand why someone would rescue a rabbit, many of the Chinese travellers would be thinking of taking it home to the pot for supper.

The little family was delighted with their new pet and named it Josan, which means "good morning" in Cantonese. Everyone saw this as a way of immediately doubling their knowledge of Cantonese by saying "Josan"! Deciding that, as they lived in an apartment, keeping Josan in a cage was not a good idea, Josan shared the apartment with the little family and could regularly be seen hopping in and out of the chairs, sipping Tsing Tao beer from the tops of visitors' cans on the warm, balmy nights spent entertaining.

Visitors rubbed their eyes in disbelief, as they at first imagined they that they had seen a white rabbit hopping around, only to realise that it was indeed a giant white angora rabbit who had a liking for Chinese beer. They found it very amusing as Josan worked his way from one beer can to another, he became distinctly wobbly on his feet, and his left ear would droop. Home visits were well sought after, as Josan became quite a celebrity. Her husband could regularly be heard saying that Josan did not set out to be an angora rabbit, but because he ate an angora pullover, he became one. Constance avidly disputed this!

Constance also introduced visitors and friends to Bonzer, the family rescue dog who came from the streets with only his lovely brown eyes. The family immediately fell in love with Bonzer, who eventually became a celebrity, as he had a wardrobe of bow ties, each grander than the one before. Constance laughed when telling friends that the children had started using their weekly pocket money to buy the bow ties, the latest being a huge blue one with white spots that he wore for swimming. Sadly, this went limp as soon as it hit the water. His grandest was a black velvet one, which set off his white bib beautifully for the more formal occasions when the family entertained. He also wore the black velvet one when he joined his family on formal occasions and when visiting neighbours for supper parties.

Being a family of animal lovers in Hong Kong, the children were always on the lookout for animals that needed their help and refuge, and there were many. On one occasion, the children came home with a sheepish look on their faces, telling everyone that they had saved a cat from being hit by a car. They decided to name their latest addition Tiggy. Rescued from the street as a tiny, wretched creature, Tiggy was only a few weeks old. The children, with Hoi Fung's approval, turned one of her rooms into a Red Cross hospital room for the new addition, setting up a rota so that there was always someone 'on duty' to care for and feed the little kitten. Hoi Fung found this amusing, telling the children, now dressed in nurse outfits, that she had never seen this sort of thing before! The children had put a big red cross on the door during the little cat's recovery period.

Tiggy became a sleek, elegant, beautiful cat who was obviously born for greater things than being a street cat.

One evening, having sat on her luxurious, padded, red Chinese chair, Tiggy watched Hoi Fung setting a beautiful table for their imminent supper party. Tiggy, intrigued by what Hoi Fung had spent hours doing rather than playing with her, leapt onto the formal dining table set for a dinner for visitors due within 30 minutes. Tiggy hit the table with such force that the entire contents of the setting smashed to the ground, including silver knives, forks, China, and the family crystal. This happened just thirty minutes before the dinner guests were due to arrive, but the greatest concern was Tiggy's injured foot, now carefully encased in the finger cut off a rubber glove and securely taped in place. From that moment on, everyone knew where Tiggy was, for as she walked, the glove finger bent and flipped up and down with each step, making a distinctive loping sound.

Fortunately, the waiting guests were served so many gins and tonics by Constance's husband's batman, a young soldier whose main duty was to look after his officer, while the table was being re-laid, that they decided it was the best supper party they had ever attended.

The military was somewhat transient. As a rule, postings to the Far East were for a two- or three-year period, causing much heartache as to whether pets were left behind in the care of others or taken with them on returning to the UK. The latter being costly due to the quarantine rules. Under the quarantine rules, animals from the Far East at that time seeking entry into the United Kingdom were quarantined for six months. One of the significant reasons for quarantine in the 1940s was to avoid the spread of rabies. To the relief of many military personnel, colleagues being posted in invariably agreed to take over one or all of the pets who were previously living in the accommodation. This kindness, however, did not stem the heartache of having to leave them behind.

Still on the theme of pets, one of Constance's close friends, a Japanese lady married to an Englishman who owned a tin mine, and whom her children loved to visit, had a small house-trained (or not) monkey called Puddles. He was called Puddles for a reason that will shortly become clear. Puddles was always present when visitors came, and he seemed to grow in importance with each arrival.

Invariably, he wore a little jester's waistcoat and hat, with a broad, somewhat mischievous smile on his face. Constance recalled that on one occasion, when visiting, she was alone in the sitting room with Puddles, when he boldly jumped onto the table where tea was about to be served. He proceeded to lift the teapot lid and relieved himself in it, and then coolly popped the lid back on. It left Constance thinking that this was probably why tea always tasted somewhat different when visiting that particular friend, noting that she would opt for cold drinks in future!

Constance was pleased to discover that the education for children in Hong Kong was of a consistently high standard, largely thanks to the mix of nationalities in each class and the diverse backgrounds of the teachers themselves. This was enhanced by the learning that took place simply from living with and being influenced by many different nationalities and cultures.

Constance was amazed when one day her four-year-old daughter started responding to Hoi Fung (the amah) in Cantonese! The children learned to speak Cantonese with ease as they spent a great deal of time in the company of Hoi Fung.

Constance was occasionally taken aback when she heard Hoi Fung muttering what were clearly Chinese swear words, especially given the frequent chaos she encountered while entering the children's room to clean. Constance just had to hope that if the children started using these words in school or elsewhere, not many of their friends would know what they were saying!

Hong Kong had an eclectic mix of nationalities; the majority (92%) were Chinese, and a significant proportion of the Chinese population were descendants of migrants from other parts of China. Constance understood that this was especially true after the Chinese Civil War in 1927, which led to a mix of Chinese, Filipinos, Indonesians, and people from various European countries settling in Hong Kong.

Socialising was high on the agenda during the time the family spent together in Hong Kong. Babysitting was readily available in the form of Hoi Fung, who saw it as an honour to take care of the children while their parents attended Mess functions.

Mess life was excellent, with a Sergeant's Mess for the non-commissioned soldiers and an Officers' Mess for those who had advanced and received a commission granted directly by the UK Monarch. Mess nights were a regular occurrence, providing wives with the opportunity to wear their beautiful long evening dresses and finery, many of which were created by the best Chinese tailor in town. To the amusement of many, the tailor was fondly known as Mr. Sew and Sew by the military families who, when leaving Hong Kong, would leave their measurements with Mr. Sew and Sew, knowing that at any time in the future they could contact him and have a new suit made and shipped to the UK. Visitors were often amazed when Mr. Sew and Sew could produce tailored suits in just twenty-four hours. It was quite a novelty for those visiting Hong Kong on holiday.

Mess Kit for the men was a soft romantic red jacket, white shirt with a stiff detached collar and black jodhpurs, finished off with a bow tie, crisp white shirt, and the then infamous George boots with spurs. The detached collar on the white dress shirts proved extremely difficult to handle on the one occasion Hoi Fung was on her one day off per year. Unfortunately, Constance had a fear of anything flying, such as bees and wasps. While heating the flat iron on the dreaded black range meant keeping the huge windows open. When deciding to tackle the collar head-on, Constance kept the non-aerosol spray starch and the non-aerosol fly spray close to hand. She heard the dreaded buzzing and quickly threw a towel over her head, aiming at the buzzing and spraying for all that she was worth. Only when peeping out from under the towel did she realise that the windows were covered in spray starch! From then on, her husband used to let people know that he had not been troubled by a bee or wasp ever when wearing his stiff collars since!

CHAPTER SIX

Constance recalled moments in Hong Kong, that had made the greatest impact on her and which she was eager to share with her extended family after the Hong Kong tour of duty had run its natural course. One such memory was hearing about and eventually being taken to see, the Kowloon Walled City. The Walled City was densely populated, noted at one time as the most densely populated city on earth. She learned that it started out as a fort, lending itself to the creation of the Walled City.

The structure had its own self-governing rules and served as a refuge, albeit one that worryingly included active criminal elements. Drugs were plentiful, and to the thirty thousand or more people living there, they were seen as an easy escape from the harsh realities of life, a life many believed they would never escape from.

The Walled City sat on the tip of mainland China in an area called Kowloon. Kowloon (Nine Dragons) took its name from a legend that says one dark moonlit night, nine fishermen's sons were playing in the sea when they were transformed into nine dragons that went on to live and roam in the fields and mountains surrounding the area forevermore.

Venturing into the Kowloon Walled City without a knowledgeable guide was certainly not recommended, Constance recalled being told. If permission were granted, visitors would face a network of narrow alleyways with staircases, allowing those who knew their way around to move from north to south without touching solid ground. Constance learned from a missionary who had obtained permission to enter the Walled City that the issues within it seemed to reflect the ongoing Sino-British tentative relationship. Constance was moved by what she saw and heard, which linked to the support that outsiders were striving to give.

Assistance was being provided to residents by charities and other religious groups who worked to help residents improve their living conditions. The Hong Kong Government provided them with access to water and basic mail delivery. However, help offered was frequently met with resistance, being viewed as interference. Seeing the plight of the young children living in the Walled City, Constance resolved that should she ever find herself in such a position where she could help disadvantaged children in the Far East, she undoubtedly would do so. On leaving the Walled City, she made a cash donation to the charity that worked tirelessly to support its inhabitants.

Constance felt a tremendous affinity with the issues that the residents of the Walled City faced. She could see some similarities with the structure of her hometown of Londonderry, which is well-known for its grand, well-preserved city walls, noted as a defining feature of the landscape. Constance recalled how Northern Ireland also had a long history of sectoral tensions and violence, much like the regular unrest in the Walled City. So many similarities, she mused, yet on opposite sides of the world.

CHAPTER SEVEN

After much daydreaming, Constance returned to the current challenge with a somewhat lackadaisical shake of her head; her thoughts returned to escaping the clutches of the Japanese Army. Whilst deep in thought, Constance heard a voice.

"Nei Hou missie! (Hello mother) You come with me la?"

The small Chinese figure, dressed entirely in black, waved frantically for Constance and her children to join her on her tiny sampan, which rocked precariously on the murky onshore waves of Repulse Bay.

As the little group tentatively approached the beach, it was getting a little crowded. Several Chinese men and women had appeared after learning of the escape plans, quite possibly through the Chinese Amah network, and had come to the beach to help the gweilos (non-Chinese) escape by using their sampans to get the travellers off the beach. If they could do this, they were hopeful of getting them to ships that were waiting to take escapees around the island to the harbour, from where they could pick up an ocean-going liner taking them finally away from Hong Kong and to safety.

"Mei, mei!" (younger sister) could be heard, and "Me po" (old grandmother) Chinese ladies called out to assure the young families that they were no threat. "Nei Ho, Nei Ho!" (hello, hello) the Chinese lady called to other families. Gradually, the scene on the beach revealed many sampans with their fearful Gweilo passengers swaying on the waves as they made their way out to the dark, mysterious, vast, and silent open water of the South China Sea.

Coming back to earth and feeling momentarily reflective, Constance recalled the relationship she had had with many of the Chinese people who worked in and around Stanley Fort. She was aware of the need to respond with politeness and respect to the woman calling to her whilst swaying back and forth on her flat-bottomed boat. Being aware of the way in which the old Chinese lady was helping the group, Constance called, "Gei Ho, gei ho! Dorjay, dorjay!" (Hello, hello, thank you, thank you).

The Chinese lady seemed unaware of the strange picture she made as she rocked back and forth on her sampan, quite used to the native wooden, keel-less boat and its foibles. Invariably, sampans had been hand-made using an old, reliable pattern that had been used for centuries in the Far East by fishermen and those hawking small products for sale using their boat.

The Chinese lady's three-plank, homemade boat was her livelihood, and tonight she was using it to help "Gweipos," or white non-Chinese women, escape the terror of the approaching Japanese Imperial Army and reach safety.

Constance felt queasy, but the children, despite their fear and tiredness, thought it great fun, despite the decidedly fishy smell due to the fishing nets scattered around the boat that had no doubt been used for fishing that day.

The children peered into pots and pans, all of which smelt totally fishy. The old lady spoke to the children, smiling at their interest. "Sic faan?"(eat food) she asked them with a hint of laughter in her voice. With this comment, the old Chinese lady was asking them if they had already eaten, as she would have gladly shared her potential evening meal with her little passengers.

Constance felt a moment of worry as all three of them had eaten very little that day, caught between excitement and fear. Fortunately, the children responded with "doh jeh moh," meaning thank you, but no thanks.

CHAPTER EIGHT

Having waited for what seemed like an eternity, bobbing up and down on the waves, the most amazing image appeared as if out of nowhere, as if in some incredible dream. Riding the offshore winds with ease, a majestic Chinese Junk bearing the grand name *Shangdu* came into sight, sailing silently through the blackness of the night with its fine linen sails and glittering Chinese lanterns draped around its perimeter.

Totally magical. It sat silently, as if waiting just for them. Constance and her little family were spellbound and speechless; the sight was nothing short of magnificent, the most wonderful and awe-inspiring thing Constance had ever imagined seeing, she thought.

A sailing ship of unknown origins, junks, she had been told, had been adopted by many Chinese fishermen for their seafaring activities and home life, being known as the safest seafaring vessel for many centuries.

The *Shangdu* sailed majestically into view, using its linen sails arranged like a Venetian blind to guide the beautiful vessel a little closer to the Bay, where Constance and the other little families were nervously waiting, sitting precariously on sampans, to see if this magnificent junk, like nothing they had ever seen before, would allow them on board.

After bobbing back and forth to get close to the side of the *Shangdu*, with the help of the old Chinese lady and the Chinese sailors, the little family clambered safely on board the wondrous, beautiful vessel.

As Constance stepped onto the junk, a tremor ran through her entire body. It brought with it a strange sense of safety, a quiet assurance that she had made the right decision to flee, even though the feeling was laced with deep sorrow at leaving her husband to the mercy of the Japanese Army.

She simply had no idea when or even if they would ever see each other again. With every breath in her body, she prayed that they would, somewhere and somehow, be reunited to continue their lives together. The children did not appear to understand the magnitude of what was happening in Hong Kong. Constance and her husband had taken care to ensure this was the case, hoping the children would leave with happy memories rather than those shaped by the fear and uncertainty the adults were facing.

Constance stopped for a moment and turned to give the old lady an unexpected hug. The old Chinese lady was momentarily speechless but hurriedly returned to the beach to help other "Gweipos." Constance thought she imagined little tears trickling down the kind old lady's face. It was unusual for a foreigner to give a local Chinese person a hug. How very sad, thought Constance, as the entire family had grown close to Hoi Fong, their Amah, who had disappeared after hearing of the approach of the Japanese Army.

There were tears from the Chinese lady, and tears from Constance, as she remembered how readily Hoi Fong had come to their rescue when it became clear that she and her children needed to leave Hong Kong for their own survival and safety.

Hoi Fung had packed up her small number of belongings the evening before, when Constance told her they were going to try to escape. At the same time, Hoi Fung told Constance that she would take Tiggy, Bonzer and Josan to her home in China and promised to look after them until their lives naturally ended. Constance parted with several small items of jewellery to help Hoi Fung with the upcoming costs of taking care of the children's much-loved pets. The children were heartbroken, thinking that they could put them into their cloth bag with their other cherished items.

Sadness was somewhat tinged with gratitude as the children had come to love Hoi Fung and knew she would look after their pets. They asked several times why Hoi Fung was unable to join them in escaping from Hong Kong. Constance explained that Hoi Fung had her own family at home in China and had to return to take care of them.

Having clambered aboard the magnificent junk, the children were captivated by its grandeur and quickly struck up a friendship with the Chinese sailors, who were intrigued by their fair skin and their genuine love and respect for family.

On board the *Shangdu*, navigating around the coastal shores of Hong Kong Island was no mean feat, especially at night, and the sailors entertained the children with colourful stories of how they used their 'wet' and 'dry' compasses for navigation in the choppy inshore coastal areas.

In broken English, the sailors kept the children amused with stories of how they kept out of the way of the Japanese Army, sailing cautiously with no lanterns burning at night, as the

Japanese invasion was happening at the time that the *Shangdu* was taking people to safety. Little did the sailors know that the Japanese Imperial Army would soon occupy Hong Kong for the next three years and eight months.

The children learned from an old Chinese sailor, who had the most amazing gold teeth, that the compass, which responded to the earth's magnetic force, could be floated in water (wet) or fastened by a silk thread to one of the beams (dry) to help guide the junk safely around the coastline. He told them in Pidgin English that the Chinese compass always faced south, as south was where good fortune was to be found, explaining that they must always move forward and never stand still.

The ancient seaman had a little bird in a tiny bamboo cage. Further entertaining the eager children, he carefully opened the cage door and encouraged the little bird to come out. The old seaman laid out some cards on a rickety old table fastened to the deck of the *Shangdu*. Each card bore a Chinese character, and he encouraged the little bird, which did not attempt to fly off, to select a card for each child. He told the children that the cards had foretold they would be lucky and live long and happy lives. Having carried out this wonderful task, the little bird hopped back into its cage, using its beak to close the cage door gently after being given a little treat for its good work.

The children sat back in amazement, confident that this would be the case, as they had no real sense of failure. Like their mother, they had an inbuilt store of confidence and determination, even at their young age. Young dragons stirring, perhaps, thought their mother. Their pedigree of courage and resilience knew no bounds, reflecting on how their aunt in

Londonderry had met and married an American airman, becoming one of the first 'Flying Nightingales'.

Constance explained to the children that their aunt had joined a group of other women, all of whom regularly risked their lives by flying out to war zones to treat injured soldiers. Working as part of the Women's Royal Air Force (WRAF) and taking their name from the famous Florence Nightingale, they used specially adapted planes to fly injured servicemen home to hospital, earning them the name, the Flying Nightingales.

Having reflected on the life, she had left behind in Londonderry and in Hong Kong, and realising that she now needed to call forth her dragon, hop on its back for strength, and get herself and her little family to safety; Constance believed that somehow the *Shangdu* would play a significant part in that.

The children were used to being in the company of indigenous Chinese men, women and children and this proved to be extremely useful while on board the *Shangdu*.

Using their limited knowledge of Cantonese, the children asked countless questions of the Chinese sailors and discovered that the young Chinese children on the junk had been born and raised there, never having set foot on land. They travelled the mystical South China Seas with their families, fishing, or moored off Aberdeen Harbour during times of rest and for the many festivals celebrated there.

Their sea legs impressed the English children, who played with them, climbing over fishing nets and rods, and bouncing on their little rolled-up beds, which were brought out at night for the children to settle down for sleep.

Constance was fascinated when walking cautiously around the junk to check on the children. She came across a small garden with six beautiful, small trees.

Sensing her delight and surprise at seeing trees growing on the junk, one of the Chinese crew, who all seemed terribly old to Constance and the children, explained that they were Chinese orange trees, being grown as New Year gifts for their families on shore.

In her short time living in Hong Kong, Constance had learnt that the beautiful Chinese orange citrus trees symbolised good fortune and were thought to bestow luck and prosperity on the recipients. It was believed that the greater the number of fruits on the tree, the greater the luck and good fortune for the recipient.

One of the Chinese sailors lifted a small sapling out of a pot and wrapped it in cloth, which he had soaked in water. He gently handed it to the children, saying that if they looked after it, it would bring them endless good fortune. The sailor went on to tell them that the orange tree would grow to about three feet tall, almost as tall as themselves, he joked. He explained that they should remember that a young tree was called a sapling, just as a small duck was called a duckling, and therefore, they must always take great care of it.

The children stood in amazement that such a beautiful little tree could be growing on board a ship. They lovingly carried the sapling, chattering to each other about what they would plant it in so that it could travel safely with them.

"Mummy, Mummy, look!" cried the children as they carried their precious treasure to show their mother. Constance thought how very kind the Chinese sailors had been to them, realising she might never have the chance to repay their generosity.

To her surprise, Constance heard a deep, warm voice speaking to her from the shadows. It told her that the trees were to be part of the upcoming Chinese New Year festival, when all their families would come together to celebrate the Lunar New Year. The voice continued, explaining that the Lunar New Year was the time when wives and mothers thoroughly cleaned their living areas (including on board the junk) to brush away ill-fortune and make way for good fortune.

The warm, somewhat hypnotic voice went on to say that much celebration would take place, bringing families together, and that his crew and their families would celebrate the upcoming Chinese New Year on board the *Shangdu*, his mighty junk.

Constance was a little spellbound, wanting to ask questions, but sensed that it was not expected of her. She hurried to find the children to tell them a little more about the beautiful Chinese orange citrus trees.

"If my family could see me now!" thought Constance with a wry smile to herself. She thanked her internal dragon for helping her get to this stage of her long, arduous journey.

The journey on the Chinese junk and its kindly crew felt both magical and healing, as they were treated with great warmth and respect. The sea, though dark and at times unsettling, remained calm as they sailed close to the shore, carrying them safely towards the main harbour and the next stage of their journey.

CHAPTER NINE

Little did Constance know that the captain of the junk, called Shangdi, was a Chinese Sea Lord, well respected in Hong Kong and immensely wealthy. Constance was mesmerised when she looked up and felt the presence of Shangdi. He stood before her, legs akimbo, his dark eyes shining and seeming to reach out to her. His crew looked on in amazement as their Sea Lord spoke to the Gweipo, the non-Chinese lady. Constance thought she was in some wonderful dream or trance. Never had she felt such a strong pull, realising that here was the Pearl Dragon, a 'Dragon of Dragons', a person with unimagined, boundless forethought and understanding of others.

It explained why the junk was so well managed. Shangdi understood what drove all his crew, and therefore, how to get the best out of each of them. The crew of the *Shangdu* felt a tangible love and respect for their Sea Lord, which was evident throughout the time Constance and her children spent on board the majestic Chinese junk.

It was clear that Shangdi would need no introduction to the Hong Kong Harbour Master, who oversaw the great liner that hopefully was to take Constance to her next place of safety. They had learned that this would be the Philippines, which at that time was considered safe.

The Chinese Sea Lord had remained quietly in the background during the journey, nodding respectfully to Constance, noting the closeness yet firmness she demonstrated when dealing with her children. The hairs on the back of her neck bristled whenever the mighty Sea Lord was close by. She was alarmed that she did not need to see him to know that he was there. Constance considered herself a realistic individual, so she could not quite understand the impact her time on the Chinese junk was having on her. She reflected on how time spent on the junk was also broadening her children's view of life in general. They, too, had never come so close to seeing and understanding how life was so different for Chinese children in such situations.

Constance believed her children had grown in many ways during their short time immersed in the lives of those who spent their entire existence aboard the majestic *Shangdu*. She realised that what she and her children had learned would surely make them better people, having experienced and understood things they would never forget. She saw the first sight of a dragon appearing within each of her children and was delighted.

The colourfully decorated *Shangdu* sailed majestically and silently through the murky waters with the evacuees on board, eventually entering the busy but exciting Hong Kong Harbour. The junk slipped silently between the famous Star Ferries and the flotilla of small Chinese fishing boats, which slowly and shakily made their way across to Ocean Terminal, where many of the ocean-going ships were frequently moored. Good business could be conducted with passengers disembarking from the huge liners.

Notable were the Star Ferries, a fleet formed in 1888 by the Star Ferry Company to provide a scenic way of traversing the waters between Hong Kong Island and the New Territories, which sat on the northern tip of the Chinese mainland.

The Sea Lord, Shangdi, so named in honour of the god of victory and war, was a figure of formidable power and renown among the harbour authorities. Descended from an ancient line of Chinese nobility, he carried himself with the quiet dignity of his heritage and was ever robed in magnificent Dragon Garments, embroidered with a host of celestial dragons that seemed almost to move with life.

On arrival into Hong Kong Harbour, Shangdi went on board the huge ship, the *Empress of Japan*, which was destined to take Constance and the other weary travellers on the next stage of their uncertain journey to safety. Shangdi advised the ship's captain that he wanted to introduce his Gweilo, (his non-Chinese family), whom he would vouch for and entrust to the captain of the *Empress of Japan*. The ship's captain was instructed to ensure that after Constance and her children left Shangdi's care, they would survive and take with them much joss, and good luck.

The families felt understood and totally respected and were in many ways sad to leave their new friends. "Dorjay, Dorjay," they called to the crew of the mighty Junk to thank them for their help and care.

With Shangdi's blessing, the family groups led by Constance boarded the amazing ship, catching up with many friends who had left earlier on one of the Filipino lighters arranged by the British Government.

Before leaving the junk, however, Shangdi asked if Constance would accept a gift from him. Concerned though she was at accepting a gift from a man other than her husband, she hesitated. However, Shangdi spoke in the most respectful way:

"Had I met you in another life, Constance-Philomena, you would be my number one wife, and your children would be my children. My Chinese name for you is Moon Flower, a beautiful, intriguing, mystical flower that may appear only once in a lifetime. While aboard my treasured junk, I have come to recognise your strength and determination as a fellow dragon and wish to present you with a piece of jade. This stone represents wisdom, which you possess in abundance, harmony, which is a strength in you and your family, and protection, which I hope accompanies you wherever your travels may take you. Go safely knowing that I too am thinking of you and your safety and will do so until the end of time."

Constance was overwhelmed and deeply touched by the kindness and sincerity with which the wonderful gift was given. She knew that no matter what she faced in the future, she would always remember Shangdi and his total majesty. Indeed, she had an unearthly feeling that at some time in the future they would meet again. She instinctively reached for the small red silk ribbon she had in her hand, having only moments before removed it from her daughter's hair and handed it to Shangdi.

Shangdi was somewhat taken aback, but even though hardly any words had been spoken by Constance, he seemed to understand the significance of such a gesture. He took the precious red ribbon and tucked it into his Dragon Robes close to his heart for safekeeping.

Constance reflected on the magnificence of the jade, having learned previously from Hoi Fung, her Amah, that the deep blue-green jade was the most precious of the jade colours available. It was known as Imperial Jade and was extremely well sought after.

CHAPTER TEN

On board the grand *Empress of Japan*, now recommissioned for carrying evacuees, Constance and her fellow passengers were elated yet somewhat disappointed to find total confusion. After the serenity of the wonderful Chinese junk, this was starkly notable. They quickly learned that, unfortunately, the passenger lists provided to the Bursar responsible for the boat's passengers were inadequate and somewhat haphazard, having come from many different sources.

Constance was delighted to find that she had been allocated a cabin for herself and her children. Realising that not every family was as lucky, she wondered if the jade might be helping! Perhaps Shangdi had implored the captain to give Constance and her family some level of preference. However, she immediately invited another little family to join her.

She felt fortunate, as many passengers had only camp cots close to each other on the decks and in different parts of the ship. It seemed to Constance that every available space had been turned into a sleeping area. Luck prevailed, as the allocation had been done alphabetically; Constance had a surname beginning with 'B'. The mighty ship eventually set sail on its journey to the Philippines.

One of the first things the children asked their mother to do was to find a pot in which they could place the sapling given to them whilst on the mighty junk, the *Shangdu*. Constance was given a small pot by one of the sailors, allowing the children to plant the little sapling. She hoped against hope that, with a miracle, she would be able to see it grow from a sapling into a fine Chinese orange citrus tree that eventually she would be able to share with her relatives in Londonderry at a time to coincide with the Chinese New Year.

The *Empress of Japan* sailed smoothly through the South China Sea, passing the Luzon Strait between Taiwan and the Philippines, and eventually reaching Manila, the capital of the Philippines. The islands, situated in Southeast Asia on the eastern edge of the Asiatic Mediterranean, were steadily gaining recognition as a developing and strategically vital region, their people and resources linked far and wide through trade and investment.

Yet, unbeknown to the travellers aboard the *Empress of Japan*, the islands were already marked on the map of the Japanese Imperial Army, destined for future occupation. Once again, it was the wealth of natural resources that made the Philippines a prize, and a shadow of danger now hung over the unsuspecting passengers as they sailed toward their fate.

Life on board the ship was relatively stable, with children enjoying games on the decks and exploring areas of the vessel that were not prohibited. Mothers kept a calendar of the days, ticking them off, looking forward to whatever life in the Philippines would bring. The Philippines had been chosen as the nearest relatively safe place to Hong Kong or so it was believed.

CHAPTER ELEVEN

Much to the delight of the passengers on board, the journey seemed to have passed quickly when three days later the Empress of Japan docked in the Port of Manila. They were hoping for some semblance of freedom and time to think of what the future held for them.

After disembarking from the huge ship, passengers then faced a six-hour train journey, taking the exhausted families to their Red Cross-provided accommodation. Travelling on a huge black diesel train, clanging along on the rickety rails, belching smoke, caused one child to comment on it being like a dragon she had seen in her reading books in Hong Kong.

Their destination was Baggio, a highland city nestled in a mountain range in northern Luzon, famous for its beautiful pine forests and its rich cultural background; this was to be home for the weary travellers. High in the mountains, Baggio was celebrated for its pleasantly temperate climate, a welcome relief that the travellers instantly appreciated after their long journey, breathing in the crisp, refreshing air with a sense of renewed energy. Their accommodation, the Loretta Hospital, was provided by the Red Cross, who immediately set about providing warm food and most welcome cold drinks. Constance, her children, plus the little sapling were made to feel as comfortable as possible.

Loretta Hospital was home to the weary travellers for a little over five weeks and was warm and welcoming. Constance introduced herself to the Mother Superior and the team of

Catholic nuns who ran the hospital, identifying herself as the informal leader of the group from Hong Kong. She was delighted to hear that the nuns who ran the hospital had education as a top priority on their agenda, encouraging Constance to work closely with them to form informal groups to facilitate the establishment of a school for the children.

This was well received as it immediately brought structure to the day-to-day life of everyone. Wives and mothers were expected to help the nuns around the hospital. The following five weeks sped by and it fell on Constance to explain to fellow travellers that word had been received indicating that the Japanese Army, having captured Hong Kong and Singapore, were now heading towards the Philippines to take advantage of its strategic position and its wealth of natural resources.

Once again, it was deemed necessary to relocate the evacuees to safer areas. Constance thought long and hard about the next move, knowing the risks that others in her group had chosen to ignore. Many believed they could build a life in the Philippines for themselves, their children, and their husbands, if they were fortunate enough to survive the horrors of the Japanese prisoner of war camps. The weight of that possibility pressed heavily on her as she considered every choice with care.

They had learned that very few British military personnel who had been captured in Hong Kong were still in Hong Kong; most had been taken by ship to Osaka, Japan to reside in the huge, dreaded prisoner of war camp there. Those in Hong Kong were forced to provide support to the invading forces, working against the goodwill of those still living in the Colony.

As the group were forced to leave the hospital for the next stage of their epic journey, Mother Superior took Constance to one side, telling her how sad they were at their departure. She added that having the children around the hospital had brought fun and happiness to everybody during what had been a challenging time. Little did Mother Superior know that further difficult times lay ahead for the kind Loretta nuns. Constance reflected once again on having made another influential friend under extremely difficult circumstances… The jade, yet again she wondered!

CHAPTER TWELVE

Sad to be leaving the relative tranquillity of the Nuns' care, Constance and her companions found themselves once again aboard the Empress of Japan, bound for the next perceived, safe port, Melbourne, Australia.

Their thoughts were with the Nuns, praying that they would survive the invasion threatened by the Japanese Army. Sketchy news indicated they were moving closer to capturing this lovely country and its beautiful people.

Reflecting on what would be another epic sea journey , since leaving her husband and the children's father behind to an uncertain future, was totally daunting and all-consuming. Constance spoke to her internal dragon, the source of her strength, and at the same time found solace in the cold but beautiful jade stone. Not knowing what was to come, her thoughts drifted to her husband. In some ways, Constance felt stronger having met Shangdi, the majestical Sea Lord. He seemed to have believed in her and increased her inner strength.

Australia at this stage of World War II was viewed as reasonably quiet and would, it was hoped, provide the evacuees with a feeling of tranquillity and relative safety to sit out the war, however long that may take.

The evacuees were initially cushioned when first arriving in Melbourne by the superb support provided by the Australian Red Cross. On arrival, the Red Cross initially housed them in empty military buildings with rows of bunk beds for people to sleep on. In addition, military chefs cooked and provided substantial but basic meals for the many hundreds of evacuees. The kindness of the Australian Red Cross and people living nearby would never be forgotten.

However, top of Constance's agenda was to search for longer-term rental accommodation to get them out of their temporary shelter, realising that this was only workable and possible if she could find paid employment in what was an extremely challenging job market.

Basic allowances provided by the British Government covered only the bare necessities but were sufficient when supplemented by the Red Cross. However, Constance knew it was time to take control and create a plan for survival that would, in time, return her to Great Britain and reunite her with her husband and family.

Evacuees were advised by the Australian Government that if they wished, they could apply for citizenship and remain in Australia for the longer term, potentially bringing their extended families out from the UK to make a new life in Australia at the end of the war. To many, this was an exciting possibility!

An easy option was not something Constance could afford to consider. The close family ties (represented by the red ribbon) that bound her to her extended family were a massive draw for Constance to eventually make her way back home to the UK. She fervently believed that she would be united with her husband to create a new life together. Little did Constance know that a letter was on its way to her with bad news about her husband. Communication was limited and managed to the best of their abilities by the Red Cross and the military, but sadly, things were happening that Constance knew nothing about.

Bringing herself back to the task at hand, Constance knew that to be free to take up employment, she needed to find a school for her children.

When Constance heard that a family-run grammar school in Melbourne was looking to expand its boarding facilities, she sent a letter filled with hope to the school.

Mentone Grammar was a Victorian, independent Anglican Grammar School in a suburb of Melbourne. The school appeared benevolent to the evacuees, encouraging Constance and several of the other evacuees to find solace in the help that the school offered to them and their children by setting up special funding arrangements to ease the financial burden. Information sent to the evacuees let them know that Mentone Grammar School boasted a beach bathing hut, a swimming pool, and a host of other sporting activities! The children were highly excited at the thought of sun, sand, and fun when going to school! One was heard to say, "It even has beach huts!"

At the tender ages of four and seven, Constance found it difficult to make the heartbreaking decision to be parted from them, knowing they would feel homesick and that she would miss them terribly if they were to board at school

She pondered on what seemed to be one of the biggest decisions for her to make thus far. Even though the children were very young, they had no way of fully understanding the impact boarding at school would have on them and their mother.

Once the decision had been made, Constance established that the cost of a place at the school was 30 shillings per week per child. This was a significant amount. However, it covered tuition, board, laundry, stationery, and gymnastics. Further costs were needed for pocket money and toiletries. The school agreed to a weekly or monthly settlement arrangement.

Anticipating that the mothers of the young evacuees would need to work during the school holidays, the school also confirmed that the children could stay at the holiday house annex on the premises during these times.

Planning for and eventually attending school brought a level of excitement, as many young evacuee friends were joining at the same time. Constance was frequently reflective of the trials and tribulations she and her little family had been through, but what she faced in parting with her children caused so much heartbreak to her, it seemed almost too hard to bear.

"It took all my strength to make that decision. However, it was truly the only thing I could do to help us survive." Constance-Philomena grew wistful, thinking of the power and strength she felt from the beautiful, cool green jade stone given to her by the Sea Lord Shangdi aboard the majestic and mystical Chinese junk, the Shangdu. At times, the beautiful stone seemed to become alive, almost forcing her to take hold of its magnificence.

Having decided on schooling, Constance set her mind to two things: securing a job and moving out of the Red Cross hostel-type accommodation into rental accommodation. She was informed that Moonee Ponds, an inner-city suburb in Melbourne, would be suitable. Situated within the city of Moonee Ponds government area and characterised by its historical mountains and magnificent parklands, with reasonable access to Mentone Grammar School, the area was ideal.

With accommodation arranged, Constance set about finding paid employment. It seemed that the only job on offer for the unskilled female evacuees was working in a munitions factory.

This sector had opened its doors to female staff when large numbers of men were drafted to serve in the war effort.

Over time, Constance found that working in a munitions factory in the 1940s in Australia was repetitive and physically demanding. At times, it was quite dangerous, as it often meant working long hours with a high risk of accidents due to the hazardous materials being used. Working in such an environment for periods of time caused a yellowing of the skin from exposure to TNT. As a result, the female workers became known as the "canary girls"!

CHAPTER THIRTEEN

Constance was feeling quite exhausted, working 12-hour shifts, plus whenever she had the time, she visited her children at school, usually accompanied by other mothers who found themselves in the same bazaar situation. The effort to cope was at times soul-destroying, made more intense when reflecting on the safety of the prisoners of war.

At times, Constance found herself thinking of Shangdi as she gently caressed the cool, beautiful jade stone, wishing it could somehow bring her news of her husband.

She found it heart-breaking when the children asked when they would see their father. This was something Constance could not bear to think about.

In the darkness of the long night, when alone in her bed, Constance found herself wondering what had become of her husband.

Word eventually reached her through the Red Cross, passed on from an amateur radio operator who had intercepted messages from prisoners of war. This confirmed that many men having been captured in Hong Kong had been put in prisoner-of-war camps, first in Hong Kong, where they were forced to support the colony's infrastructure, and later transported by ship to camps in Osaka, Japan, for final imprisonment until the war ended.

When talking to other evacuees as they worked operating the huge, noisy, somewhat dirty machinery, chatter generally turned to what they would all do when the war finished. Several were determined to stay in Australia, taking up the generous offer of gaining citizenship for themselves and their husbands, which had been offered to all evacuees.

Exciting as this prospect was, as it would bring immense stability to her turbulent life, Constance still felt the strong pull of her family in Northern Ireland. So many things went through her mind in the empty darkness, but in her heart of hearts, she knew where her future had to be, and that was back home in the arms of her family with her husband.

This thought kept her going through the many lonely hours she spent when she was not working or sharing hugs and smiles with her children during visits to the school. Constance's heart broke every time they asked when they could come home!

However, Constance was simply elated when, unexpectedly, she had the opportunity of hearing the voice of her wonderful husband! The voice disk message, followed by a written version, reached her via the Red Cross, who had received the communication from a group of amateur radio users who had picked it up whilst listening in one evening to general chatter on the airwaves. Constance knew nothing whatsoever about amateur radio buffs! However, she was simply delighted to be able to play the disk on a battered old recording machine in the offices of the Red Cross and hear her husband's voice.

The boost was significant, and Constance was delighted to be able to let her children hear their father's voice too, sending them all his love. Constance reflected on how she was not truly alone, as her husband had been thinking of her and her children, and the Red Cross had been searching for news to pass on to them.

"Bonds of love helping to carry me through," thought Constance. Oft referred to was the red ribbon that, no matter where she was, bound her to her extended family. She shared the concept of an internal dragon with fellow evacuees, who were amazed by her notable strength and determination, asking her if this was why. One claimed being amazed at the determination and strength that Constance demonstrated when an issue arose affecting all of them.

Occasionally, a telegram bearing urgent news arrived. One such telegram brought the news that Constance was dreading. It confirmed that her husband was among those captured by the Japanese Army and was being transported to a prisoner-of-war camp in Osaka, Japan.

In her heart, Constance believed that the gesture made by the Sea Lord Shangdi, in giving her the beautiful jade stone to keep her and her children safe, was also intended to help her husband survive the war. If it had been Shangdi's true wish that she be forever happy, then he would know this was to be in the arms of her husband, the father of her children.

Life had settled into some sort of normalcy for Constance and her little family, but after 18 months, news was coming through that Australia was now also facing the threat of invasion by the Japanese Army. The threat of war in Australia, plus an influx of several thousand American troops, was placing incredible pressure on food, products, and services for everyone.

This situation forced the Australian Government to introduce a system of rationing. As Australian men were conscripted into the war effort, women gradually took their places, joining the evacuees working in munitions factories. Many felt that this marked a significant shift in workplace dynamics.

Constance was alert to the threat and the additional hardship that was coming her way. Many evacuees immediately chose to apply for Australian citizenship and make Australia, with its sand, sun, and vast landscapes, their permanent home. The Australian Government advised this group to move further into the mountains for safety to sit out the remainder of the war.

Constance's resolve remained strong. She never lost her burning desire and determination to return home to be with her husband and family.

Having to leave Australia and therefore facing yet another epic sea journey, Constance thought long and hard about this journey compared to those she had encountered previously.

This was the journey that, with a good tailwind, would finally carry her and her children home to Northern Ireland, a moment that would remain in her mind forever.

Constance liaised with the British Government agent and the Australian Red Cross to secure passage for herself, her children, and those of the evacuees who wished to return home to the United Kingdom. She was informed by the British and Australian Red Cross that there was a plan to transport several thousand evacuees on board a requisitioned troop ship, and even though it was still wartime, they would endeavour to get them safely home to the United Kingdom.

She learned that they planned to travel by a somewhat circuitous route to avoid the many German U-boats still active in the Atlantic.

.

CHAPTER FOURTEEN

With no choice, Constance and her fellow evacuees began what they hoped would be their final long, arduous sea voyage. They were advised that accommodation was limited due to the high number of evacuees involved.

True to their word, evacuees found the ship overcrowded, with camp beds filling every available non-working space, including the outside decks.

Constance was alarmed by the complete lack of privacy for everyone. Only her thoughts were totally private, and in the privacy of her ever-active mind, she longed to see her husband, hoping against hope that he would survive the war and come home to her and her children at the war's end.

Sadly, Constance had no way of knowing that as she began her sea voyage home in September 1942, her husband was already aboard the 70,000-ton Japanese prisoner-of-war ship, the Lisbon Maru, on its way to Osaka via Shanghai.

Constance at that time also had no way of knowing that the Lisbon Maru was about to be torpedoed by a USS American Submarine called the Grouper. The prisoners of war were split into groups of 50 and put in the hold of the Lisbon Maru at the first sign of fighting. The Americans on board the Grouper had no way of knowing that the ship housed some 2,000 non-Japanese prisoners who, at the first sight of trouble, had been locked down in the lower decks to stop them escaping.

Reports indicated that it took the American submarine two attempts to sink the Lisbon Maru: one submerged during an extremely bright night, and secondly, the following morning, when they successfully executed a surface attack, totally crippling the Lisbon Maru and causing it to slowly sink.

Constance was later to find out that the crippled Lisbon Maru initially landed on a sand bank, giving some prisoners a chance of escape by jumping into the sea.

Thankfully, when one Japanese officer realised that the ship was sinking, he unlocked the hold, allowing prisoners to escape the ship. Many drowned or were shot in the water by a nearby Japanese warship, while some were rescued by the islanders of Sing Pang Island.

The inhabitants of Sing Pang, Constance later learnt, had played a crucial role in rescuing many prisoners of war from the sinking ship as they floundered in the water, undernourished and weakened. They were also suffering from dysentery and malnutrition. The villagers took the prisoners they saved to one of the biggest and most overgrown of the islands in the Sing Pang group, to give them cover and places to hide.

Even though they were themselves suffering from a lack of food and nourishment, the villagers shared what little they had with the prisoners, offering them food, water, and places to hide when the Japanese Army came searching, as they eventually did.

However, by this time, the prisoners were given valuable aid by the villagers, so felt stronger. Others had been hidden by the villagers on uninhabited islands and out of reach of the Japanese Imperial Army. Unfortunately, more than 1,000 prisoners, including the husband of Constance, were recaptured by the Japanese from the water and continued their journey on a second Japanese ship, condemning them to life until the end of the war in a brutal Japanese prisoner-of-war camp in Osaka, Japan.

Such catastrophic news would eventually find its way to Constance via a telegram from the British Government whilst she was on her journey back to the United Kingdom. Meanwhile, Constance and the other evacuees were themselves met with shortages of food and support on board the requisitioned ship. Hearing the journey could take five to six weeks, Constance came to the fore and spoke to the bursar and sailors on board to arrange safe 'site' seeing tours of the ship for small groups of children. The Bursar agreed, knowing that bored children would be harder to control on board the crowded ship.

Children could be heard excitedly chatting about being taken down to the boiler room, feeling the heat and smelling the steam as they learned that this was the powerhouse of the ship.

Laughter could also be heard as younger children held races, jumping from bed to bed, creating havoc in the living accommodation provided for them.

Children spent much of their time collecting bits of rope so that the sailors could teach them to tie knots, and they also played, often precariously, in the lifeboats secured to the outside of the ship.

Towards the end of the war, passenger sea travel between Australia and the UK was, not surprisingly, significantly impacted by World War II.

Frustration was felt at the frequency of unscheduled stops to take other passengers on board, who were fleeing their own dangers. This naturally placed additional stress on services being provided to an already overcrowded vessel sailing against all odds. The high number of passengers pushed the boundaries of what the ship could safely provide. However, Constance knew they were all in the same boat literally so all pulled together, moving camp beds a little closer, encouraging children to top and tail.

Camaraderie was at its height and appreciated by all.

The typical route to Australia from Britain was via the Suez Canal, with stops in Colombo, Port Aden, and Port Said. However, wartime conditions could alter routes and necessitate longer voyages, hence manoeuvring the huge ship around the Bay of Biscay. Constance and her fellow travellers knew full well how lucky they were to be heading home, even though they faced daily risks associated with the war playing out around them, including potential attacks from submarines.

To relieve the potential stresses from impacting too strongly on the children on board, sailors spent as much time as was feasible providing them with some sort of entertainment. They explained the 'ship's bell' system, for instance, calling it the 'seven bells.' The children learnt that the ship's bell made everyone on board aware of the time. They eagerly returned to their mother, advising her that a bell would go off every thirty minutes. The seventh bell was destined to advise the sailors to prepare for the next shift, so stand by.

They had learned that the seven-bell system was a long-standing seafaring tradition observed by sailors of all nations. The children had also asked why sailors wore wide bell-bottom trousers and discovered that the design allowed someone to easily grab the trousers to pull a sailor out of the water if he fell overboard.

Constance was amused to hear her children telling other children in their sleeping area to keep everything 'ship shape and Bristol fashion,' meaning neat and tidy.

Feeling curious, Constance asked why Bristol fashion. She was told that it was named after the rigorous maritime systems that the busy Bristol Docks were known for.

Life at sea was challenging and at times tortuous due to persistent rough seas, which seemed to last for days and days. The ship was cramped and the confined somewhat claustrophobic environment made everyone on board feel restless uneasy and nervous. This was especially so for the children, who unless active became restless and a little out of control. However, Constance was filled with pride at the adaptability demonstrated by her children since their evacuation from Hong Kong. She thought to herself, how long ago that seemed.

CHAPTERFIFTEEN

While still on board the overcrowded vessel, Constance received a note from the bursar, who handled administration and the ship's post. Feeling concerned, she left the children in the care of another mother and made her way to the Burssr's office.

The ship's captain was also present and was holding an important-looking telegram.

The captain asked Constance to sit down, as he had some very important news for her. The telegram expressed sincere condolences from King George VI on the sad death of her husband, who had passed away in the prisoner-of-war camp in Osaka, Japan. She was told that death was caused by dysentery, malnutrition, and a disease called Beri, all brought on by the appalling conditions in which prisoners were kept.

Constance felt overwhelmed with grief and physically collapsed into a chair. The Bursar brought her what he called a 'strong tot' (of rum), which he told her each sailor on board was given at 11 a.m. each day.

The captain advised Constance to sit for a while and compose herself before facing her children with the heartbreaking news that their much-loved father had died.

She was advised that the formal notification from the King would no doubt be waiting for her on arrival back in Londonderry, as that was her last known permanent address. However, some very thoughtful soldier at the Ministry of

Defence had taken it upon himself to try to locate Constance and her family. All recommissioned ships carrying evacuees were required to maintain a full manifesto detailing passengers travelling with them at all times, and this was how the unknown soldier had located Constance.

Constance, undoubtedly aided by her dragon left the bursar's office and returned to the hall, where the children were being entertained by a group of evacuee wives and some American sailors travelling with their families to the UK.

Telling her children of the sad news of their father's death was the most challenging thing she had ever had to do apart from leaving them at boarding school on that first day. They were naturally heartbroken, but children being children, as soon as their friends called for them to come and practice tying knots with big pieces of rope provided by one of the sailors, they went to join them, only returning to their sadness at bedtime.

Constance felt bereft as never before, but knew that for the sake of her children, she needed to stay strong and get herself and her children home.

Constance frequently spoke to her children about the bonds (the red ribbon) that kept them close even when apart, and the dragon inside each of them, letting them know that if they believed, then their dragon would raise its head to help them when they were afraid or unsure. She also regularly made the point of talking to her children about their father, their home, and their family in Londonderry. To the children, home was a world away, and they were correct yet again, for they would travel halfway around the world to eventually get home to Londonderry.

Constance was aware that during 1942, Londonderry had played a major role in the Battle of the Atlantic. German U-boats were endeavouring to interrupt the supply route to the United Kingdom, bringing a range of supplies. The city became an important staging base for American, Canadian, Indian, and French troops, creating a wonderful, vibrant culture.

However, returning to her journey home, after what felt like an endless voyage, the enormous ship finally arrived at Queen's Docks in Glasgow. Back on UK soil at last!

Whilst delighted to be touching dry land, Constance looked in awe at the sight that greeted her. After six weeks at sea, she felt totally drained and lacking in emotion. She dwelt on how all the children on board had grown in stature and understanding during their epic journey.

Queen's Dock was a wonderful sight; local people had put out streamers to welcome the evacuees home. The docks, built in 1870, were recognised as a major central shipping hub. Constance and her fellow travellers looked out across the city from their vantage point while still on board the ship. They could not believe the devastation that met their eyes.

They marvelled at the way Glaswegians had organised a small welcoming party, insisting on helping the women and children make their way down the gangplank to touch dry land after a journey that had tested almost all their resolve. Many, with weak and wobbly legs after such a long sea voyage, were grateful for the assistance.

Constance noted the lack of men among the small crowd that greeted them, having been told that, due to the intensity of the war and the impact on the dockland, almost every able-bodied man had been called up to join the war effort.

As they left the ship, the children scanned the gathering to see whether any local children had come to watch the huge ocean-going liner pull into the docks.

"Where are all the children, Mummy?" one little voice asked.

Constance remembered the letter she had received from her friend, explaining that children were being evacuated from Londonderry to the countryside to escape the devastation of war. Sad though this seemed, Constance knew that countless children had faced similar upheaval, her own included.

CHAPTER SIXTEEN

Having finally disembarked the vast and overcrowded ship, Constance faced the next stage of their journey: trains to Manchester followed by a train to Liverpool and then a ferry across to Northern Ireland . After so many epic sea voyages since leaving Hong Kong, the prospect of a train and ferry felt almost welcome. She reflected on how far she had travelled since she left Londonderry to join her husband in Hong Kong many years ago. Now she and her children were almost back where they had started.

The first stop was Manchester, a great metropolis in the North West. A similar sight greeted them there, with widespread devastation surrounding the busy station. There was no welcoming party not that she had expected one, she reminded herself. Next would be Liverpool, the ferry, and then home. Could this really be happening, she wondered. So much water had passed under the bridge since she left her hometown supported by her loving family. Now, so near the end of her long ordeal, she felt a sudden doubt about whether she was truly so close to home and to the familiar arms she longed for.

Feeling exhausted and low in spirit, Constance allowed her thoughts to drift to the short but unforgettable time she had spent aboard the beautiful and mysterious Chinese junk, the Shangdu, and her brief and extraordinary encounter with the mighty Sea Lord, Shangdi. She kept the beautiful jade stone close to her body at all times. Its presence gave her confidence that some greater power was helping her to survive for the sake of her children.

When they arrived at Liverpool Lime Street station for the final stage of their journey across the Irish Sea to Londonderry, Constance was again shocked by the scale of wartime destruction that greeted them at every turn. She realised she should not have been surprised, as every place they had passed through so far had been a major industrial centre and therefore an obvious target for German bombers.

CHAPTER SEVENTEEN

Constance was unsure what she would find when she arrived home, for on 3 September 1939, Derry's once peaceful existence had come to an end when war was declared. Events unfolded that changed everything familiar to her and her family. By that time, Constance was married, had two children, and was preparing to join her husband on what had been described as the posting of a lifetime. Before she left, she remembered how Derry, or Londonderry, had seemed to disappear at night from the air as the blackout was imposed. All street lamps were extinguished, making once familiar streets unrecognisable. This, together with strict food rationing and coupons issued according to the number of family members, added greatly to the strain felt in the approach to war.

At family gatherings, Constance often remembered the stories of black-market coupons, for ration books were regarded as gold dust. For weddings, birthdays, or even for new clothes, it was always helpful if extra coupons could be borrowed from relatives willing to share what little they had.

During her darkest days working in the munitions factory in Melbourne, when she had neither her husband nor her beloved children to talk to, she sometimes smiled to herself as she recalled how resourceful her relatives in Derry had been. Despite rigorous rationing, the town's close proximity to the border with the Irish Republic, which was then a neutral country, enabled intrepid members of her family to cycle towards the border, bypass customs, and return with what could only be described as black-market goods. They would often leave with shopping lists from family and friends, especially when weddings, Christmas, or other special events were approaching.

Her thoughts drifted to the day her sister announced that she was to marry an American serviceman and would become known as a GI bride. Constance asked what GI meant and was told that it referred originally to the American indexing system, Government Issue, and later came to describe American servicemen. The Americans stationed in Northern Ireland enjoyed a comfortable life with no shortage of goods or facilities, all provided by the United States, regardless of where their personnel were deployed.

At that time, Constance and her family learned that the British and American press were always eager to report on these international romances, often seeking photographs of the weddings for publication in newspapers on both sides of the Atlantic. It was believed that some seventy thousand such romances and marriages took place. The press was especially delighted when they heard of a GI bride 'telephone wedding' taking place. These ceremonies became a unique wartime tradition. They were not simply matters of convenience but a response to the many challenges created by wartime separation.

The Americans brought a sense of permanency to the area rather than simply passing through like other foreign troops. Large and well-equipped permanent stores were established, supplying American personnel and, for those with the right connections, offering access to luxuries otherwise unavailable.

Goods and equipment were brought directly from the United States. If Constance's memories were correct, before she left for Hong Kong, there had been an abundance of sweets, candy bars, ice cream, and tins of pineapple chunks, all courtesy of the US Marines and their own GI bride.

When Constance eventually returned home after her long and arduous sea journeys, she found Londonderry settling into a form of normality again, although the changes affected some people more deeply than others. Constance was now a widow with two children to raise on her own. When she first arrived home, she and her children moved in with two generations of extended family, thereby becoming the third all living in a terraced cottage

Warships had departed from the docks, which once again became idle and quiet. Many lives had been changed forever. Constance was alarmed to see that post-war Derry faced rising unemployment and deepening poverty. Northern Ireland's industrial economy had suffered greatly. Constance and her family felt fortunate that, although their own lives had changed significantly, their strength and mutual support had remained. She smiled when she recalled how fourteen members of the family had shared a small house on the Waterside in Londonderry when she first arrived back from Hong Kong with her children.

Feeling more secure, Constance and her children settled into a new 'normalcy' supported by her many relatives who were eager to help in any way they could. She found so many things had changed during her time in Hong Kong and in the

Philippines and Australia. It was, however, still 'home' and provided her growing children with new experiences.

Employment opportunities in Derry remained limited, and many young men chose to join the military to see the world. With her encouragement, Constance's son enlisted in the British Army, choosing to pursue the opportunities and stimulation available beyond his hometown. Constance was delighted, for it told her that her son had found his drive, or his dragon as she fondly called it, and that he was taking control of whatever the future might hold. Little did she know that one particular posting of his would open unexpected opportunities for Constance.

CHAPTER EIGHTEEN

In the fullness of time, Constance was given the opportunity to return to Hong Kong to spend time with her son and daughter-in-law, as her son had been posted there on a tour of duty with the British Army. With a mixture of excitement and emotion, she set off on her long journey, flying by super jet from London directly to Hong Kong. She reflected on how very different this trip was compared to her first and second journeys to the Far East.

The jade stone had travelled with her on a chain around her neck. In some ways, Constance felt a twinge of disappointment in herself. Her thoughts kept returning to the first sighting of the majestic, mystical junk that had sailed into view so many years before, seen as a saviour to the evacuees waiting on the beach. A flood of emotions swept over her, the same she had felt when she accepted, with some trepidation, the cool, beautiful jade stone from Shangdi. At that moment, she felt a closeness to him, trembling inwardly at the memories she had carried for so long.

As part of her visit, Constance returned to Repulse Bay Beach, the place where she had held her children's hands and fled from danger. In her mind's eye, she saw the old Chinese woman on her home-made sampan, waving kindly as she had that night. How kind the woman had been, ready to help; perhaps she, too, had recognised the affinity Constance felt for her and what she represented. Those memories of fear and uncertainty remained as vivid as ever. Ironically, her son and daughter-in-law now lived in a luxury apartment overlooking the very bay from which she had escaped so long ago.

Constance also revisited the Walled City in Kowloon. With greater understanding than before she empathised deeply with its inhabitants and the life they endured.

Constance reflected on how during her holiday to Hong Kong, her son and daughter-in-law had arranged for her to visit Stanley Fort, where she and her young children had spent two memorable years with their father. The experience was emotional, stirring both joyous and sorrowful memories. She stood on the coastal path, gazing out at the South China Sea, thinking of her late husband and the great Sea Lord, Shangdi. She often reflected on the Chinese name he had given her, Moon Flower. Intrigued by its significance, she had deliberately researched its meaning.

Constance established that the Moon Flower blooms only once a year. During the day it is no more than an inch in height, but when the moonlight touches on one night alone, it opens into a seven-inch-long magnificent blossom. Among the Chinese, the Moon Flower is considered aloof, beautiful, sweet-smelling, and romantic. Constance had learned that it must be handled with extreme care, for it is both spellbinding and somewhat toxic, linked to immortality, beauty, fragrance, and, some say, intoxication! In contemplating the Moon Flower, Constance felt a connection to Shangdi, a reminder of the mystical and enduring threads that had shaped her life.

The jade stone had travelled to Hong Kong on a chain around her neck. In some ways, Constance was disappointed with herself. Her thoughts kept dwelling on the first sighting of the majestic, mystical junk many years before, as it had sailed into view. Seeming as a saviour to the waiting passengers, Constance felt a raft of emotions, the likes of which she had not felt since she had accepted, with some trepidation, the cool, beautiful, jade stone from Shangdi. She felt close to him at that moment, hoping that others would not notice how she trembled at the thought of the accompanying memories.

Believing that, as she had matured after leaving the Far East some fifty years earlier and made her life back in Londonderry with her close family, watching her children grow up, her recall of the impact that Shangdi had had on her would have waned, she discovered that this was not the case. The sight of him standing, legs akimbo, so majestic in his Dragon Robes, had taken her breath away. Words had failed her; she wondered if the impact she felt was evident to those around her.

As her holiday came to an end, bringing with it re-ignited memories, Constance thought that this was her destiny; she was meant to return and revisit the place where her life had changed forever. "One day I will follow my dream of becoming immersed in charitable work in the Far East, as so much of my heart is still there," she vowed.

CHAPTER NINETEEN

On her return to Derry after her eventful trip to revisit Hong Kong, Constance settled back into her life at home. She shared the highlights, though not all, of her trip with her relatives, who, never having ventured such a distance, could only listen with awe. They did not seem able to understand nor envisage the richness, happiness, emotion, and sadness that she had experienced during her revisit. Constance knew that she had changed, but her family could not understand the affinity she had felt as she immersed herself in the Chinese culture and ways of life, giving her a richness of memories that she could not fully share with them. They could not understand how Constance and her children had settled into life in the Far East initially. Her children's friends were from diverse backgrounds; her children did not see a difference; they were children just like themselves. However, her family could not understand how they had become completely immersed in the traditions of Chinese culture, including the Chinese New Year festival, which centred on family celebrations with fireworks intended to ward off evil spirits and bring good luck to everyone.

Constance shared with her family her wish to become involved with children's charities in the Far East. Having informed them of the poverty and neglect reported within the Kowloon Walled City, she admitted that this was one place where she would have liked to offer support. However, her later research indicated that the Walled City had been demolished in the late 1990s due to its poor basic infrastructure and in preparation for the transfer of Hong Kong back to China at the end of the ninety-nine-year lease.

Conscious of the need to create a stable base for herself and her now adult family, Constance eventually found a small but beautiful cottage in North Wales. The location allowed her to be close enough to extended family for support, yet provided her immediate family and herself with a 'family base' in which to reflect, grow, and rebuild some semblance of permanency

With time on her hands, as the children had flown the nest, Constance began to focus on ways she could utilise the strength, determination, and kindness she had experienced during her time in the Far East. Despite the many arduous travels of her earlier life, Constance felt she was strong enough to venture further afield again. Firstly, she wondered if there was a way to arrange a meeting with Mother Teresa of Calcutta, a person she had greatly admired from afar for many years. Constance had read that Mother Teresa became a Catholic nun at the tender age of eighteen and lived and worked in India for some seventeen years, providing help to the poor of India.

Constance felt both compassion for and a connection to Mother Teresa, who was primarily known for her dedicated humanitarian work with the poor and marginalised, particularly in Calcutta, India. Mother Teresa also founded the Missionaries of Charity, a Catholic religious congregation that expanded globally to serve the needy. Much admired and revered, these tireless efforts earned her the Nobel Peace Prize in 1979.

Constance also felt the need to make a third trip to the 'Pearl of the Orient', her beloved Hong Kong. She found planning her visit totally invigorating, leaving her feeling that her inner dragon was on this occasion 'joining' her rather than giving her the strength to climb mighty mountains!

However, spurred on by her desire to know more about the love and compassion demonstrated by Mother Teresa and the Missionaries of Charity, Constance planned to visit India first and then travel on to Hong Kong.

Arriving in India in the smog that hung heavily in the Calcutta air, Constance was unable to miss the widespread poverty before her. However, having contacted a friend in India in advance of her trip, she was both excited and apprehensive, as indications were that she might indeed have the opportunity to see Mother Teresa.

Her first thoughts on arrival in Calcutta amazed, delighted, and yet appalled her. False teeth and spectacles were readily available on the pavement wherever she looked. They were there to try on, and if they fit, the teeth or glasses would find a new owner. Whilst this amused Constance, she reflected on how, for some of the poor, they had no other options available to them.

Children approached her taxi, begging for a little money as she made her way from the single-storey, shed-like Calcutta airport. However, her Indian taxi driver, a thoroughly polite and friendly man, advised her not to hand money through the window, as it was very likely that another hundred children would join the queue.

Constance found the people of India to be gentle souls, many with a ready smile despite having very little in terms of necessary commodities. She was alarmed when passing a street with at least two hundred men, women, and children who appeared to have been driven to protest. However, the taxi driver pointed out that this was a daily occurrence. He added, "They come out early in the morning to see who needs some protestors, irrespective of the cause, and will simply march from one street to another, supporting whichever cause will pay them the most."

Despite initially feeling somewhat despondent, Constance was very excited when her Indian friend contacted her, confirming that there was an opportunity to make a short but informal visit to see Mother Teresa. Overcome with emotion, Constance felt overwhelmed by the warmth and love that Mother Teresa showed to the little children around her during the meeting. Constance and her friend were in a small group that was given the chance of a lifetime. They waited nervously for her arrival, unsure how they should or would react when faced with Mother Teresa.

Constance found her brief encounter with this amazing, incredibly tiny, and beautiful woman overwhelming; she could neither speak nor move. Feeling glued to the spot, she held out her hand, only to feel a gentle, fleeting touch that seemed to send warmth throughout her entire body. Tears flooded her eyes, causing her to feel somewhat embarrassed. However, when she looked around, others in the small but extremely privileged group clearly felt the same.

Departing from Calcutta, she realised how deeply she had been changed by all she had heard, seen, and experienced. After leaving Mother Teresa, she resolved to provide lifelong support for the Missionaries of Charity. Constance wondered

how she could ever find another experience that would impact
her so profoundly.

CHAPTER TWENTY

Sad at leaving India, Constance set off for her third trip to the Pearl of the Orient, Hong Kong. How strange it was to arrive low over Kowloon on a vast 747 at Kai Tak International Airport. At that time, the 747 was the largest plane in service.

Flying so low over Kowloon City, Constance could almost see directly into the 20-storey apartment blocks, giving the impression that those on the ground could count the rivets holding the plane together. People on the ground thought the plane would touch the roofs, whilst those on the plane felt convinced they would land on top of one of the apartment blocks that stood cheek by jowl beneath them, each seeming to be claiming its own small piece of land on which it stood

Constance was told there were two approaches to Kai Tak Airport: one over the sea, where the runway jutted out precariously into the South China Sea, and the other over Kowloon. She looked out to see if she could spot and recognise the Kowloon Walled City, which had so impacted her emotions when last visiting, but, as she was later told, it had been destroyed in 1990 as part of the British-Sino agreement.

The impression of Hong Kong in the early 2000s was so unlike the Hong Kong Constance had left in 1945 and 1974. Change was dramatic. The Walled City had gone, and the wooden shanties sitting precariously on the hillsides had disappeared. These were replaced by block after block of 20 or even 30-story high apartment blocks, a high proportion of which were provided as part of the Government's housing scheme. Hong Kong now also boasts a Mass Transit Railway and a cross-harbour tunnel linking the island to the mainland, leaving the Star Ferry crossings purely as tourist attractions. The cross-harbour tunnel had opened to serve the ever-increasing population of Hong Kong.

Smart hotels, unlike anything Constance had ever seen before, lined every corner. She had chosen the Peninsula Hotel for her stay. It sat on the Kowloon side, gazing across the world's most exciting harbour towards Hong Kong Island, where Constance had once lived with her husband in Stanley Fort. The Peninsula prided itself on being the only hotel in the world to operate a fleet of eight green Rolls-Royce luxury cars, whisking its privileged guests around Hong Kong in style.

Constance felt that she was on a journey of self-discovery, exploring the fascinating Chinese culture that had captivated her for so long. Feeling uncannily at home, she began to explore. As part of her exploration, Constance hopped on a Star Ferry from Ocean Terminal on the Kowloon side to cross the harbour to Hong Kong Island. The ferry chugged slowly across, following the route that had been established many years ago as the only way of crossing from Kowloon to Hong Kong Island.

Being a Sunday, the ferry was busy, primarily with tourists who gazed with wonder as the many tall buildings appeared into view. On one side, she saw North Point, a predominantly Chinese enclave with mile upon mile of 10-storey blocks of flats, all identical in appearance, some of which, as previously mentioned, were provided as part of the Hong Kong

Government's housing programme. While chatting with a local man on the ferry, she learned that many flats housed families of ten or twelve people. Three generations often shared one apartment. She also knew that while many Chinese people chose to live in small apartments, they displayed their wealth by owning boats and modern cars, many of which were built and imported from Japan, America, and the UK, not China!

Constance enjoyed talking to her fellow travellers on the Star Ferry, hearing the general gossip of life in Hong Kong. Among the many topics she heard about from Mr. Tang Yue Fung, her Chinese fellow traveller, was the Triads; Chinese gangs whose primary income came from stealing expensive cars. Wealthy Chinese often favoured high-quality cars such as Jaguars, Rolls-Royces, and Mercedes-Benz. Constance was amazed to learn that car thieves used Chinese junks to blend in with other traffic in the harbour. Behind the junk, they would tow a huge underwater sack made of tough polythene to house and hide stolen cars, getting them invisibly transported out of the Colony and into the South China Seas to various locations around China.

Departing the Star Ferry, Mr. Tang Yue Fung guided Constance to walk along the Hong Kong Island waterfront. She gazed in amazement at the huge Meccano-like building that housed the Hong Kong and Shanghai Banking Corporation. Immediately adjacent to HSBC, as Constance entered the Central Square, she was taken aback by the sight of at least 300 Filipino women gathered on this one day of the week to talk about home and their families, many of whom they had not seen for two or three years, or even longer. In Hong Kong, it was common practice for Gweilos, non-

Chinese, families to employ a maid directly from the Philippines, contracted under Government law for two to three years, responsible for children and all aspects of housekeeping.

Constance knew that wealthy Chinese families preferred to employ a Chinese Amah instead. Reflecting on this, she thought of the help and support provided by Hoi Fung, her Hakka amah, when she had first gone to Hong Kong in 1942.

Being back in Hong Kong brought many memories to mind, including how easily Constance and her family had fitted into the Chinese culture.

She recalled being invited by Chinese colleagues to join them for 'breakfast', only to arrive at the Chinese restaurant and enjoy a twelve-course Chinese meal complete with a snake head offered to her as the privileged guest!

Feeling no unease about being in Hong Kong alone on this latest trip, Constance ventured up to an area known as Mid-Levels, where many wealthy residents lived. The high humidity in the Colony created a low-lying blanket of grey fog. It was acknowledged that the higher one lived on Hong Kong Island, the clearer the air, allowing residents to enjoy the many beautiful harbour views and its mix of exciting shipping styles. At night, Constance saw the harbour in all its full beauty, like a fairyland with countless twinkling lights on display.

A mode of transport used by many to reach the mid-levels was the Peak Tram, which operated up and down the mountainside using a cable. Known locally as the cable car, Constance jumped on one going up to the mid-levels. Here, she caught a small minibus, which took her to Victoria Peak, the highest point on the island. It stands 552 metres high, providing unparalleled panoramic views of this exciting city. The small minibuses that ran up and down The Peak were a favourite of the many Gweilos (non-Chinese) living and working in Hong Kong. Leaving their busy offices down in Central's commercial and financial district, they would meet friends and colleagues who regularly used the minibus at the same time each day. They viewed the minibus ride as crucial, enabling them to relax after perhaps a twelve-hour day on the Hong Kong stock market, called the Hang Seng. Millions of dollars were made and lost in the dealing rooms of the Hong Kong and Shanghai Banking Corporation (HSBC). The legacy of the popular minibuses was such that when it was suggested to cancel the 6 pm bus, travellers clubbed together and bought it, leaving it in the control of the Peak Tram Bus Company.

Constance spent her last evening having supper in The Peninsula Hotel, choosing a table by the window so that she could, possibly for the last time, look out over the magical Hong Kong harbour. The emergence of a huge, majestic junk caught her eye. Could it possibly be the mystical Shangdu? Emotions flooded her very being. If only… No, perhaps not. Constance was never quite sure whether she would ever cast her eyes on Shangdi, the Sea Lord who had impressed her so much with his pure majesty and magnetism.

She watched the junk make its illuminated way along the entire length of the harbour from north to south. However, she was puzzled when she asked the waiter if he knew the name of the impressive junk currently sailing across the harbour. The waiter checked but said he could not see any junk in the harbour at that time, suggesting she might have been mistaken. Constance, however, knew she was not mistaken. She had experienced an out-of-body moment that transported her back to the mighty, magical Shangdu and the majestic Sea Lord, Shangdi. Perhaps for the last time, she thought?

Departing Hong Kong was a sad event for Constance, as she felt a deep affinity for the place and its people, believing she was taking many new and renewed memories with her. With mixed emotions, she headed to Kai Tak Airport and her twelve-hour flight home. As the pilot welcomed passengers on board the aircraft, he advised them that the flight would be approximately twelve hours with a good tail wind. Constance thought it seemed unbelievable as she once again recalled the arduous six-week journey of her first ever trip to the Pearl of the Orient.

Whilst onboard the huge jet, Constance marvelled at the size of the aircraft. Sitting in the top lounge, she pondered her trip to the Far East, thinking that this would no doubt be her last time in the Orient. She flicked through the channels on offer on the small TV screens adjacent to her seat. With a glass of cold, crisp champagne in her hand, she mused across the various films and documentaries on offer, opting for one that depicted the unique and somewhat bewitching customs and beliefs of China. Moving from topic to topic, she let the channel take her wherever it would, guided by memories and intrigues.

She mused on the concept of an Anglo-Chinese marriage. The programme indicated that interracial marriage in China was a relatively recent phenomenon, with the number of such marriages increasing over time. In the past, it had been uncommon and sometimes even discouraged, but it now seemed to be more readily accepted. Indications were that before the 1990s, inter-racial marriages were seen as unusual in mainland China. The programme highlighted how, over time, attitudes had shifted, and the practice was more readily accepted, with women being more dominant in this regard.

It was, Constance understood from the programme, notable that the highest proportion of mixed marriages involved mainland Chinese women and men from Hong Kong, Macau, and Taiwan. Increased ease of travel, trade, and cultural exchanges of students had led to a big rise in interracial marriages. The changing world was demonstrating that such unions provided access to better opportunities and, thus, a different lifestyle for many.

Constance was unaware that she had slipped into a peaceful slumber whilst watching the programme. She felt herself once again on the mighty Shangdu, the majestic, magical Chinese junk which had played a crucial role in getting her and her children to safety on board the Empress of Japan. In her dream, Constance listened intently to the words spoken by the magical Sea Lord, Shangdi. In her slumber, she had the confidence to reach out and touch the hand proffered by Shangdi. She took hold of the cold, green jade stone which, during the flight, had hung on a chain around her neck.

Awakening to the air hostess asking if she was ready for breakfast, Constance opened her eyes with a look of bewilderment.

"Are you comfortable, madam?" asked the air stewardess, noticing the confused state Constance appeared to be in.

"Absolutely fine, thank you. Have I been asleep long?" she asked.

"Several hours," was the reply.

She reached for the jade stone; it felt real. Constance mused that not all of it had been a dream. At that moment, the wheels of the huge aircraft touched down. Once again, she was back home leaving part of her heart behind!

CHAPTER TWENTY-ONE

Constance had much to share with her children and her extended family, telling them how Hong Kong was now a modern, bustling, exciting metropolis and how it had once again left an imprint on her heart and soul. She noticed how her children were keen to hear every detail, understanding the magic that was the Far East. Her relatives were glad to know she had returned safely, but they could not fully understand the warmth, energy, and excitement that Constance shared with her children when describing her most recent Far Eastern visit.

Life settled into a type of normalcy, with Constance sharing in the excitement of her children as they grew and began to build a life for themselves. Londonderry was no longer the central focus for Constance. Her children were spread far and wide. To remain within reasonably easy access to them, Constance decided to remain in North Wales, to live out her life near the sea and the beautiful terrain that the region had to offer. When people previously asked why Wales, she replied, "The other land of the Dragon."

The sights, sounds, and stunning scenery of Wales provided a superb backdrop for Constance to reflect on her rich life, and she found nothing unusual in road signs written in two languages. She revelled in the opportunities to visit her children. Aside from her son's posting to Hong Kong, which had allowed her second visit, her children still found all things Far Eastern intriguing.

CHAPTER TWENTY-TWO

Constance was delighted when her daughter, Orchid, decided to attend university in Belfast, Northern Ireland, giving her the chance to get to know her relatives who still lived in that part of the world. Orchid's chosen subject was Far Eastern Cultures and Beliefs, something that delighted Constance. She felt that her own lifetime of learning about everything Far Eastern had helped make her the person she now was.

Whilst at university, Orchid met a tall, refined, handsome boy from Shanghai called Karl Kam. She learned from Karl that Shanghai sat on China's central coast and was the country's biggest city, noted as a global financial hub. Karl Kam was born in Shanghai to a wealthy family of merchants. One of the first things Karl did after several meetings with Orchid was to invite her to join him at his parents' house in Shanghai for the Chinese New Year celebrations. Known as the Lunar New Year, it remained the most important holiday in China and in Chinese communities around the world. It is also called the Spring Festival. Using the Chinese zodiac, it is based on lunar months and invariably falls in January or February, heralding a twelve-year cycle, each year bearing the name of an animal.

Karl explained that each year bore the name of a different animal: the Rat, the Ox, the Tiger, the Rabbit, the Dragon, the Snake, the Horse, the Goat, the Monkey, the Rooster, the Dog, and the Pig. Each animal was known to bestow specific characteristics on those born in its year. Orchid bustled with excitement when telling her mother of her forthcoming trip to Shanghai, joking that Karl was eager to establish her year of birth to see if they were compatible for such an interracial marriage! All rather sudden, thought Constance.

For Karl, preparing to take Orchid to meet his parents for the first time was an auspicious occasion. To all concerned, it marked a significant milestone in their relationship, including the prospect of marriage. Orchid, being well travelled and having lived in the Far East, was aware of cultural differences. Constance had spoken to her about the importance of showing respect to Karl's parents. Orchid somehow believed that the forthcoming meeting was a significant event in the lives of both families, both now and in the future.

After a thoroughly enjoyable visit to meet Mr. and Mrs. Kam at their beautiful villa in the heart of bustling Shanghai, Orchid felt at ease and at peace. Mrs. Kam was mesmerised by Orchid and her tales of the bravery demonstrated by her mother escaping from Hong Kong so many years ago. "She is obviously a very worthy person, with hindsight and determination," Mrs. Kam said, expressing how much she would like to meet her mother one day.

Orchid soon noticed the interest the Kam's were taking in the Chinese zodiac and much delight was felt when it was established that Orchid had been born in the year of the Monkey, giving her characteristics such as being inquisitive, playful, romantic, and intelligent. Karl's parents confirmed that he had been born in the year of the Dragon, giving him natural authority, good fortune, and ambition. Reflection on the zodiac highlighted that the Monkey and the Dragon made them an ideal partnership for a successful marriage!

Karl's parents were so impressed by Orchid, her love of family, and her inquisitive mind, which brought many questions to be answered. One such question concerned why the mighty Dragon was fifth in the Chinese zodiac and not first. Mr. Kam was impressed by such a forward-thinking question and explained the myth: many centuries ago, the Jade Emperor decided to hold a race for the animals in the twelve-year zodiac cycle. The race was going extremely well, with the Dragon firmly in the lead. However, as he flew above a village, he noted a severe drought and famine with many people starving to death. The Dragon left the race, swooped down, and with his mighty breath, roared into the clouds to make rain, saving the village and its inhabitants.

Rejoining the zodiac race, the Dragon surged towards the lead again. As he neared the finish, he saw a rabbit being chased by a wolf. He swooped down and let the rabbit go ahead, keeping it safe from the wolf. The Dragon finished fifth, just after the Rabbit. Orchid was completely mesmerised and felt a deep sense of love and compassion for Karl's parents, hoping that Karl would feel the same when he met her mother.

The Kams could see and feel how much in love Orchid was with their son, never having imagined that he would meet and marry a British girl. They had moved with the times and were indeed quite forward thinking in their views, all of which augured well for Karl and Orchid. Mr. Kam spoke at length about his father, who had also been born in the Year of the Dragon, a powerful Sea Lord who now lived in an extensive Chinese village in the north of China.

Orchid made a note to tell her mother of her incredible experiences whilst staying at the villa of Karl's parents. Whilst in Shanghai and during Lunar New Year, Karl took the opportunity to propose to Orchid. Accepting with delight, agreement was reached that the wedding would take place in England, with both an Anglican ceremony featuring a traditional white dress and a Chinese wedding, when she would be adorned in a beautiful red dress to be provided by her future in-laws. "Oh, so much to tell my family when I arrive back home," Orchid thought.

The Kams were rightly proud of their Chinese culture and lost no time in taking Orchid on a whirlwind tour of Shanghai, hoping that it might whet her appetite and encourage the young couple to make a home in China too.

Orchid's first visit to her boyfriend's parents' home city revealed a vibrant, cosmopolitan Shanghai, offering a mix of modern and traditional attractions. The City was busier than Orchid had imagined it would be, with many popular destinations for tourists to explore. As is often the case when visiting a new city, there were countless wonderful places to see, but never enough time to see them all.

Karl and Orchid enjoyed their walk along the Bund, an historic riverside promenade showcasing the city's stunning waterfront. It offered amazing views of the city's skyline and its famous historical buildings. They also paid a fleeting visit deeper into Chinese culture by exploring the magical Yuyuan Garden, with its mysterious rockeries shaped as dragons, its waterways, and its superb jade Buddha. Karl promised Orchid that they would make many visits to Shanghai if that was her wish.

The more Orchid saw and heard about China, the more she was driven to see and learn more, hence her choice of studies focused on Chinese culture and beliefs.

CHAPTER TWENTY-THREE

Life was progressing well for Constance, who enjoyed living near the sea, often musing on how the sea had played a massive part in her life and her experiences. With time on her hands, she frequently thought back to when she had first met her future husband in Northern Ireland and how she and her sister would love to don their finery and head out into town.

She recalled a funny tale from their younger years, after they had both become brides. One Christmas night, Constance decided to take the car and drive to visit her sister, who was staying in a hotel. Her sister was on holiday, and the route was dark and rainy. Constance was concerned, as the little back roads were very busy. This was her first visit on her own.

Fearing she was lost, and with mobile phones not yet making communication easy, she spotted a phone box and pulled up beside it. She phoned her sister's landline. Her sister immediately took control. She asked Constance where she was and what she could see in the dimly lit side roads. Constance eagerly explained that she was near a small hump-backed bridge and added, "In a garden just across from where I'm parked, there is a huge Christmas tree with many lights on it, you can't miss it!"

In a firm voice, her sister told Constance to "get back in your car, lock the door, do not move, and do not open it for anyone until I arrive." Constance obeyed, knowing she had no way of finding her sister's hotel on her own. Her sister immediately set off in her car, confident that she would quickly be able to find her mis-placed sister!

However, five minutes later, as Constance sat waiting, she saw the Christmas tree moving down the road and realised it was on the back of a Round Table Christmas truck doing its rounds of Christmas donation collections! By this time, her sister, also driving along, saw a giant Christmas tree pass her on the opposite side of the road. She realised, with horror, that it was the Round Table's Christmas truck making its rounds!

Each time the sisters met after that, they laughed heartily, grateful that all had ended well. Constance's sister noted that she had been parked near the only hump-backed bridge in the vicinity. She collected her sister, and both set off, laughing hysterically.

CHAPTER TWENTY-FOUR

Constance frequently found herself thinking of the forthcoming wedding of her daughter Orchid and her Shanghainese boyfriend, Karl. According to Chinese tradition, the groom-to-be formally seeks the assistance of a matchmaker, who usually visits the girl's family to request their permission for the proposal. However, Karl and Orchid decided to visit Constance to ask for her permission for them to marry. Karl brought several gifts of chocolates, sweetmeats, and small Chinese ornaments.

Constance asked for a little time to discuss this important step with her daughter. Deep down, she was delighted at the thought of perhaps, in the future, having a Eurasian grandchild. She admitted to herself that she was not surprised at Karl's approach, as it is common in China for the would-be groom to meet with his future family-in-law two or three times before the formal proposal. Karl was also determined to follow the British custom of presenting an engagement ring. He had the ring safely in his pocket, knowing that his time with Orchid's mother on this visit was limited. Karl had given careful thought to the stone and style of the ring. Unaware of the beautiful, cold green jade that Constance wore around her neck, he instinctively chose green jade set in a simple red gold band.

Before Karl and Orchid left Constance's lovely home, she gave Karl her wholehearted blessing to marry her daughter. Feeling delighted, Karl produced a small, embroidered silk purse and lifted out the exquisite ring, leaving Constance breathless at the sight of the jade, the exact colour of the stone that the Sea Lord, Shangdi, had given to her so long ago.

Constance understood the significance of Karl's gesture in visiting her. In Chinese culture, a union is not just between the bride and groom but between their two families. The happy couple began planning their wedding, fortunate to have Constance and Mr. and Mrs. Kam keen to assist. All were eager to play a part in arranging a very special 'blended' wedding.

After much searching and several visits, a magical castle in North Wales was chosen as the wedding venue. Everyone was delighted, as it met all their requirements: a small church in the grounds for the ceremony, a beautiful venue for the wedding breakfast, and an ornamental lake for photographs. The castle stood on a hill overlooking the soft, golden beaches that surround the Welsh countryside.

Mr. and Mrs. Kam were overjoyed when they arrived in the United Kingdom several weeks before the wedding. A somewhat formal first meeting took place between Constance and Karl's parents, and Constance immediately felt at ease with Orchid's choice. To her, it all made perfect sense.

During supper on their first evening in the UK, Mr. and Mrs. Kam visibly began to relax, sensing Constance's affinity with the Far East. They also recognised her strength and the love she had for Orchid and believed she would feel the same for Karl in time. The families were delighted at how well they connected, looking forward to both the Western and Eastern wedding breakfasts, where Karl's relatives would join Orchid's extended family in celebrating their love.

Constance and Mrs. Kam joined Orchid for the final fitting of her traditional white dress and the red Chinese cheongsam. The intricacies of the wedding were many, but everything flowed smoothly. While sipping champagne provided by the bridal parlour, Mrs. Kam began to relax further and spoke of her family in Shanghai, explaining that both she and her husband came from large families. Constance had to swallow hard as Mrs. Kam continued, revealing that her husband's family were descended from aristocrats stretching back hundreds of years.

Mrs. Kam went on to explain that her father-in-law had been a well-known Sea Lord who had spent many years sailing the South China Seas. Constance felt an immediate warmth towards her, wondering if the Sea Lord being referred to could indeed be the magnificent Shangdi. How could that be possible in such a vast world, she wondered!

That evening, Mr. and Mrs. Kam reflected on the day in their hotel room. Mrs. Kam noted how Constance had gone quiet when she mentioned her husband's greatly admired father. Mr. Kam thought little of it at the time, believing his wife might be over sensitive. He felt at ease with Constance, observing her inner strength and her determination to provide a safe and happy life for her children, despite the hardships she had faced when escaping the Japanese Army and leaving Hong Kong Island.

Mr. Kam's revered father had told him how he and his crew, aboard the mighty junk the Shangdu, had rescued a small group of women and children fleeing the Japanese invasion of Hong Kong. Mr. Kam paused, shook his head, and thought that it could not possibly be that his father and Constance had met before, as if in another life. The timing, however, was right, as Shangdi had indicated that the rescue had occurred just before the fall of Hong Kong. He decided not to elaborate further until after the wedding.

CHAPTER TWENTY-FIVE

The wedding day arrived. Sunshine and blue sky. All good omens for a happy life, though when Mr. and Mrs. Kam drew back the heavy drapes that had kept the bright sun out, they saw that their room in the castle was steeped in history. Karl's parents eagerly sought as much historical information as possible to relay to relatives in Shanghai who had not been able to attend the wedding or be part of the wedding party.

Everything had been done to ensure the wedding was a unique blend of traditional rituals and modern practices for both families. When planning the much-awaited wedding, Constance and Mr. and Mrs. Kam received much advice and support from the wedding planner who handled wedding banquets on behalf of the Castle. She explained that she had already met one of her objectives, which was to ensure that the sun shone all day long on the happy couple and their diverse family members.

A somewhat unusual suggestion put forward by Karl had been that he and Orchid follow the Chinese tradition of dressing up in their finery two weeks before the wedding day for the formal photographs. This they had done in advance of their wedding day.

The young couple had been able to make arrangements, including capturing some beautiful photographs of themselves together in a small sailing boat on the castle's ornamental lake. For these pictures, the couple wore both their Western and Eastern-style wedding outfits to reflect their shared cultural heritage. To align East and West they arranged for a red tissue paper junk to be made to float on the ornamental lake to add colour and tradition to their wedding photographs.

The happy couple had chosen to formally register their marriage in the beautiful church in the castle grounds. In keeping with Chinese tradition, Karl's parents presented betrothal gifts to Orchid's family, symbolising prosperity and good fortune. Orchid was delighted to include the Tea Ceremony, during which the couple served tea to their parents and elders, showing respect and gratitude for all they had done for them throughout their lives.

For this part of the ceremony, Orchid delighted her new husband and parents by appearing in the beautiful red cheongsam, the traditional Chinese dress. All were aware that red was viewed as a dominant colour and thus focused on ensuring good fortune for the couple. Orchid and Karl both wore red and gold outfits, knowing that when gold was paired with the beautiful red, it signified wealth and prosperity.

Later, Constance reflected on how she had felt when Karl's father produced a beautiful, red, and colourfully decorated Chinese umbrella, which he held over the bride and groom when they said their vows. The gesture had taken her breath away in its significance, causing Constance to reach for her beautiful, cold, green jade given to her by Shangdi. She learned later that under normal circumstances, the bride's father would make this gesture. However, knowing that Orchid's father was no longer alive, Mr. Kam had taken on this extremely important activity to ensure that the couple felt safe, keeping them protected as they journeyed forward as man and wife.

The formalities were followed by a large celebration hosted by Karl's parents in line with their customs. Only round tables were used for all the guests. In the Chinese culture, banquets typically feature round tables due to their symbolic representation of unity, reunion, and harmony. The round shape (yuan) signifies the reunion of families and friends, which emphasises family togetherness and the seamless flow of conversation and shared meals.

Red envelopes containing money (lai see) were given to the happy couple by the elders to wish them good fortune in the future. To ensure good luck and prosperity, Constance had agreed to follow the fortune teller's advice, which considered the Chinese zodiac signs and birthdays of the marriage couple.

In line with the long ancestral history of Karl's aristocratic family, his father's regimental sword was used to cut the wedding cake. Constance was intrigued by the markings and beautiful designs on the handle of the amazing sword. Something about the carvings and colours on the sword caught her attention, feeling that she had seen those colours before and how they had changed her life forever. She approached Karl's father to learn more about his family background and the sword.

Mr. Kam felt at ease talking about his heredity and background, telling her that the sword was his father's and that of his grandfather before him. He went on to say that the sword had been in his family for several centuries. The current owner was Karl's father, a well-respected Sea Lord who had sailed the China Seas for many years with a fleet of huge Chinese Junks the biggest of which was called The Shangdu!

Constance felt herself feeling a little weak and disorientated. How can the world be so small, that yet again, Shangdi had a pleasurable impact on her daughter by allowing her to find Karl, whom she adored and with whom she would no doubt have children that would hold a wonderful blend of both the East and West. Constance decided not to tell Mr. Kam about her meeting with Shangdi so many years before. For the time being it was a precious, secret memory for her alone. As yet, she remained unsure that their lives could be linked more closely than anyone could possibly have envisaged!

However, Constance reflected that, perhaps in time, she would tell Orchid about her own life-changing encounter aboard the majestic junk the Shangdu. Of course, having been present at that fateful meeting herself, Orchid might retain a faint memory of the Sea Lord who had fallen hopelessly in love with her mother.

After the wedding, Orchid, Karl, and his family paid an auspicious visit to Constance's beautiful home in North Wales sitting on a hill looking out to the sea and surrounded by many far eastern plants lovingly nurtured by Constance, including the wonderful Chinese Orange citrus tree.

A unique custom dictates that on the third, seventh, or ninth day after the wedding ceremony, the newlyweds visit the bride's family home. This provides the bride's family with the opportunity to host a reciprocal banquet for the groom's family. Orchid was delighted to observe this beautiful Far Eastern tradition, knowing that at such an event they would, for the first time, be formally recognised as a couple.

In the fullness of time and after much reflection, Constance took the huge decision to visit Karl's parents in their home in Shanghai. The invitation from Mr. and Mrs. Kam was aligned with the Chinese New Year festival, which, as Constance was aware, is a most auspicious occasion. Having accepted the kind invitation, Constance, as is her way, researched the dos and don'ts of such a visit. She noted that on arrival she should firstly remove her shoes and avoid hugs and kisses – something that would feel strange to Constance. She knew that when handing a gift to the Kam's she should use both hands and, above all, not leave immediately after the meal. Constance also knew that she should avoid appearing difficult or embarrassed if the Kam's raised the issue of finances. Additionally, she was guided to greet the elders in the family first, with warmth, to show respect in line with Chinese tradition.

After much soul searching, Constance set about planning and arranging her visit to Shanghai. She felt somewhat nervous, particularly with the potential link back to the majestic Sea Lord, Shangdi. She thought, "just how can such a thing happen?" As she touched the beautiful, cold, green jade that hung around her neck, she felt nervous and excited in equal measures. In her heart of hearts, deep down, Constance had held onto the belief that somehow, somewhere her path would cross with that of Shangdi again.

Orchid shared in her mother's excitement, eagerly recounting the many visits she had made when she first met Mr. and Mrs. Kam. She once again went over the numerous mysterious and intriguing memories she had brought home with her.

Constance decided to accept the kind offer that the Kam's had made when inviting her to join them in their home.

On arrival at Shanghai Pudong International Airport, Constance was guided to take the direct train into Pudong in central Shanghai, where the Kam's had promised to meet her. Constance found the 1.5-hour train journey incredibly interesting, with so much to see. She found the Hakka workers in the paddy (rice) fields most notable. What had caught her eye were the large bamboo Hakka hats they wore. She had learned that the Liang Mao (cool hat) was the traditional hat worn by all outdoor manual workers. Accompanying the hat, workers wore a long-sleeved long dress (Shanku) that wrapped around at the front, protecting them entirely from the sun. Shankus, she knew, were invariably dark blue.

CHAPTER TWENTY-SIX

Constance was somewhat relieved to see Mr. and Mrs. Kam at the train station. Initially she had the sinking feeling that she may not recognise them in their own environment. The Kams' liveried driver transported them to the Kams' beautiful, traditional Chinese villa (a siheyuan).

She looked in wonder at the exquisite courtyard residence, featuring many interconnected buildings reflecting their wealth through its size, symmetry, and architectural features. The Kams explained that the covered courtyard was the heart of the villa, being used for large family gatherings and contemplation. They told her that, being in a financial position to do so, it was seen as their duty to provide a home to their extended family branches. Constance could see and feel the harmonious blend of the design, which carefully captured the sunlight whilst collecting gentle breezes for all to enjoy.

Constance looked around, wondering why she felt exhilarated, with a strange feeling in her chest. The Kams explained that she must see the villa as her home on this and any future visits she may choose to make. They reminded her that under Chinese tradition, their children's marriage was a marriage of both families.

Showing Constance to her room, the Kams commented that there would always be a home for her in their villa. At the same time, they showed Constance a set of rooms marked 'Karl' and 'Orchid', adding that upon their marriage, a suite of rooms had been set aside solely for the use of the newlyweds whenever they might need them.

Mrs. Kam took her by the hand and led her to a door just off the one for Karl and Orchid, with 'The Nursery' on it. She could see that Constance was looking at her questioningly, waiting for Mrs. Kam to explain. Thus far, Karl and Orchid had not started to build a family of their own, wishing to see the world in all its magnificence for themselves first The sight of the nursery set Constance thinking about how beautiful it would be if the young couple decided to start a family. Perhaps a little, mystical Eurasian girl, a child that they could perhaps call Lilly Moon Flower! The thought brought tears to her eyes, which Mrs. Kam immediately recognised and once again took Constance by the hand, leading her to the communal courtyard, the heart of the house.

Mrs. Kam said, "If at any time during your stay you feel reflective, come and sit under the lovely Chinese Orange Trees that grow in abundance and let your heart and mind come together. You will find it very healing." Constance told herself that she would do exactly that at dawn on the next morning. It was immediately clear that her daughter had joined a unique, somewhat intriguing family and that she herself was now part of that family group. She thought of Shangdi as she often did in the magnificent villa; she wondered yet again whether she should speak of her meeting with Shangdi but once again put it to the back of her mind, thinking she would wait and see how her visit progressed. Constance admired the emotional intelligence shown by Mr. and Mrs. Kam, realising that already she felt they had a platform where they could all share their hopes and dreams for the future of their two families.

After a fitful first night's sleep, Constance awoke to the warm eastern sunlight illuminating her elaborately decorated room. The room was so well aligned as to capture the sunlight, the intense darkness, and the cooling breeze. Prior to travelling to Shanghai, Constance had spent many hours researching 'ying yang' and most of all 'feng shui', knowing that to a family like the Kams they would have sought to build a house for their wider family that felt truly harmonious.

Constance knew that Feng Shui was an ancient Chinese practice aimed at creating harmony and balance between individuals and their environment. By arranging spaces and objects in a particular way it promotes positive energy, with the placement of things believed to influence a person's well-being, health, and even prosperity.

Constance felt at peace as she sipped the tea (cha) brought to her in a little ancient Chinese teapot. Having lived in the Far East, Constance understood the concept of having servants to help around the house, especially with the children. The Kams had allocated an amah called Lui Sui to care for her during her stay. Lui Sui was one of the many servants employed in the villa.

Dwelling on the restless sleep she had experienced the previous night, Constance recalled several vivid dreams. One in particular made her heart race with its realism. In it, the majestic Sea Lord Shangdi appeared before her, standing tall with legs akimbo. He held out a beautiful red silk ribbon to her, but no matter how hard she tried, she could not grasp it.

In the dream, she could hear her Chinese name, 'Moon Flower' given to her by Shangdi! It sounded so real and set all her senses on fire. It was as if he was trying to get into her mind. In the dream, Shangdi appealed to Constance to open her mind and her heart and allow him to enter.

After sipping her tea (cha), she dressed and went down to the courtyard, with its decorative Chinese Dragons, only to find that during the night, the courtyard had been decorated with red ribbons and other Chinese paraphernalia. For a moment, Constance thought it was in her honour, but as the Kams greeted her, "Jo san, Jo san" (good morning, good morning), she noticed they seemed a little subdued.

Mr. Kam was unusually dressed in a traditional decorative Chinese outfit of red and silver. Mrs. Kam spoke softly to advise Constance that during the night, Mr. Kam had received a message telling him that his father had passed away. Constance was speechless, thinking of her incredible dream. Could there really be a link? Expressing sympathy to Mr. and Mrs. Kam, she asked if her visit would in any way distract them from the funeral arrangements they were now required to make.

Mr. Kam explained that the Chinese believed in the afterlife (Diyu). He went on to say that in Chinese culture, Diyu is a realm where souls are judged on their actions in life. Their souls are held accountable for their actions, and it is seen as a transitory place to somewhere else, based on the strong desires that have not been fulfilled in life. Death was seen as a necessary journey to the afterlife, where all one's dreams and ambitions are achieved.

However, a "good death" i.e. one from natural causes, is regarded as a positive event. Mr. Kam went on to explain that his traditional Chinese family held strong beliefs in the afterlife and ancestor veneration, with souls potentially facing trials and tribulations before reaching their final judgment.

These beliefs, he confirmed, were deeply rooted in Confucianism and Taoism, with practices like ancestor worship playing a significant role in funeral rituals.

Mr. Kam's family believed that his father had had a good death, as he was known for doing so many good and gracious things for those in need of help. Mr. Kam explained that Constance should not feel uneasy if they did not talk about his father's passing, as talking about death was considered taboo and potentially jinxing in Chinese culture. This avoidance, he explained, was deeply ingrained and could affect daily life, such as avoiding gifts like clocks, which sound like "death" in Chinese.

Constance listened with interest to their explanation and how they described their father's death as a good one, noting the strength that Mr. Kam himself displayed in putting on the magnificent robes and preparing to step into his father's shoes with the utmost pride and determination to echo his father's strength and desire to help and support others.

Feeling comfortable with what she was learning about the amazing family her daughter had married into, and indeed the one she had co-joined, Constance could feel her internal dragon stirring. She realised, for the second time, that the mighty Shangdi had indeed been a Pearl Dragon, one that understood the characteristics of all other dragons and could immediately empathise with them.

So much for Constance to learn and understand. Now more than ever she observed that in Chinese culture, the family was seen as one of the most central institutions to its members. For many, their family provided children with a sense of identity. Indeed, the family was seen to contain one of the most essential foundations for all social activities. All roles were clearly defined and understood.

Constance reflected on how she had spent her life encouraging her children to be as independent as possible, building a life for themselves, knowing she was there for support if needed. Some similarities existed, but not the closeness and provision she was learning about in the Kam family. From the moment she had heard of the loss of her husband in the Japanese Prison of War camp, she had felt it her duty to instil independence in her children. However, having come from a warm, loving extended family herself, Constance realised that her daughter's life and that of her new husband were not significantly different; both came from loving, caring extended families with an inbuilt desire to support and nurture each other.

Mr. Kam sensed that Constance felt some unease having heard of the various Chinese traditions. He went on to stand before Constance and tell her that he had observed the strength she had demonstrated in raising her children on her own, getting them to a place of safety on several occasions.

He also explained to Constance that this strength and determination were qualities a Chinese man sought in a wife, and that his son had found them in Orchid at their first meeting. Constance found herself unable to speak, recalling the last time a Chinese man dressed in austere robes had spoken those words to her. Mr. Kam, dressed in his majestic Chinese robes, reminded her of his father, Shangdi. She was in turmoil, unsure whether to mention the time she and her children had met the magnificent Sea Lord aboard the magical Chinese junk Shangdu, but in the end she decided against it feeling the time was just not quite right

Constance called up her internal dragon to help and protect her from the intense emotions and confusion that she was feeling. She always hoped to meet Shangdi again, but had no way of knowing when, how, or indeed if. The closeness she had felt last evening when he had entered her dreams was almost overpowering and the feelings stayed with her for some time

She wondered whether the closeness of Karl's family would place a burden on her daughter's shoulders. The action of building a house in their Villa for the young couple would seem strange to Orchid. However, Constance felt confident that Karl would explain that what she had recently been told came simply with the hope that the young couple would, in time, provide both families with children to continue the family line.

Mr. Kam explained that had they not been able to provide a home for Karl and Orchid, they would have been embarrassed about their lack of provision compared to their peers. All they asked was for the couple to be safe and happy. "Marriage was the right step to adulthood for any child," Mrs. Kam explained.

Constance was due to stay with the Kams for ten days. As such, they assured her that the plans they had made for her visit would remain in place, as the Chinese believed that souls journeyed to an afterlife, often requiring purification and judgment for past deeds, adding that this usually took as long as 49 days. The Kams could still see some unease in Constance and assured her that ancestors were honoured through rituals and offerings when the soul had left the body, as they were believed to have a continued influence on the living; thus, they should still celebrate the important visit Constance had made.

Despite the mixed emotions being felt following the passing of Karl's father, the celebrations still went ahead as Shangdi's soul would not yet have left his body. Constance felt strange at the thought that, in some way, the Kams were indicating that Shangdi's presence could still be felt around them.

Constance was told that Shangdi had been involved in making the arrangements for his own funeral in accordance with their customs and that he had indeed selected many of the red tissue paper art crafts to be burned as an offering to help his transition to the afterlife.

Sensing the genuine interest Constance showed in the forthcoming funeral, Mr. Kam explained that preparing for the funeral, or 'fai yin', was regarded as a most important ritual, extending into the magical and mystical afterlife. He added that Shangdi was totally unafraid of moving beyond the physical world.

Among the many beautiful tissue paper crafts he had requested was a replica of his main ship, the mighty and magnificent

Shangdu. A stillness came over Constance, which was observed but not fully understood by Mr. Kam, who went on to say that the red tissue papercraft would be burnt as an offering during the funeral rites to help Shangdi traverse to the afterlife and keep him safe.

CHAPTER TWENTY-SEVEN

Chinese New Year, also known as Lunar New Year or the Spring Festival, was rapidly approaching them. This fifteen-day celebration, marking the start of a new year based on the lunar calendar, was viewed as a time for family reunions, feasting, and participating in traditional customs aimed at bringing good luck and prosperity to the entire family group.

On the eve of the Lunar New Year, Karl's family hosted a Nian Ye Fan (Evening Dinner). Constance knew from her previous time in the Far East that the Nian Ye Fan was a crucial part of the celebration, bringing families together for a large banquet. Constance was happy to join the Kam family and their many servants in the traditional 'house clean' that always takes place immediately before Chinese New Year. The house cleaning was viewed as the only way to sweep away bad luck that may be in the house. It also brought good fortune for everyone in the familial group.

Having thoroughly cleaned the Villa, colourful red decorations were used to adorn windows and doors. Something that Constance was aware of and prepared for was the tradition of giving money in red envelopes (Lai See) to younger family members as a symbol of good luck and blessings. She was also aware of the incredibly noisy firecrackers and fireworks, which were set off to scare away evil spirits and celebrate the arrival of the new year. Constance remembered the sheer terror the children had felt when, still very young, they first experienced the thunderous firecrackers in Hong Kong with their father many years ago. She pictured the long streams of firecrackers strung from the rooftops of the twenty-storey blocks in the Chinese Quarter, snaking down each building to the ground. When they were ignited, the explosion of noise was overwhelming, a chaotic roar that seemed to shake the very streets below.

Constance felt very fortunate to be in Shanghai at this time of celebration, knowing it was an auspicious time for the entire family. The Kams had invited her at that time, saying it was to make her feel part of the family. There was so much going on during the many celebrations that she thoroughly enjoyed the colourful, energetic lion and dragon dances, which were performed in the courtyard to bring good luck and ward off evil spirits. The noisier, the better. Bringing the Chinese New Year celebrations to an end, the Lantern Festival marked the conclusion of the fifteen-day New Year celebrations.

Wherever she looked, Constance could see illuminated lanterns around the Villa, giving it a magical, illuminous feel. Accompanied by a ready supply of traditional foods like tangyuan (sweet glutinous rice balls), it was being enjoyed by everyone. Something that Constance had not heard before were the taboos on the first day of the new Lunar New Year celebrations, which included washing clothes, lending money, and cleaning the house. Constance enjoyed that taboo, as household chores held no fun for her!

Constance had a truly wonderful holiday with Mr. and Mrs. Kam. They were highly attentive hosts and introduced her to many of their extended family who had been unable to attend the wedding. She felt a deep sense of relief and joy as she was met with respect and warmth, reassured that her beloved daughter, Orchid, was in safe hands with this family. She was

certain they would guide and nurture both Karl and Orchid as
they grew together.

CHAPTER TWENTY-EIGHT

On arrival home in North Wales, Constance received a note from Orchid and Karl asking if they could pay her an urgent visit. Excitedly, she agreed, as she had so much to tell them about her incredible visit to Shanghai. After recovering from her jet lag following the smooth twelve-hour flight from Shanghai, as well as the exhaustion and exhilaration of being part of the Chinese New Year celebrations, she prepared for her daughter and son-in-law to arrive.

Constance had so much to tell them over a typical English meal of roast beef and Yorkshire puddings, which she had lovingly prepared, hoping that in some small way she could repay the kindness of Mr. and Mrs. Kam.

Orchid was blooming. So much so that it took Constance's breath away. Karl looked happy and contented and, in some ways, more confident, standing even taller than previously. Constance reflected on how Mr. Kam had told her that marriage is the first step to adulthood, and adulthood seemed to suit Karl.

After a lovely meal, allowing Constance to tell of her amazing trip to Shanghai and how she felt that she had been totally accepted into the Kam extended family, she recounted the suite of rooms in the villa that had been built and prepared for Orchid and Karl. Before leaving for home, Mrs. Kam had asked Constance to describe them to the young couple. They listened eagerly as Constance gave a detailed account, even sharing a photograph she had taken so they could see their charming, independent room opening onto the villa courtyard. She also made sure to mention the Nursery!

Constance saw knowing looks passing between Karl and Orchid. Holding her breath, she waited for the news that they could no longer wait to share with her. Orchid was expecting a child. Their first scan had shown it was a girl. Constance was over the moon and thought back to her musings in Shanghai, when she had wondered if they would have a girl child. Perhaps they would call her Moon Flower, knowing that the Eurasian child would be as beautiful, delightful, mysterious, and engaging as her namesake.

They hugged and cried with absolute joy, considering themselves incredibly lucky. Karl stood ten feet tall, knowing that he was in the process of thanking his amazing parents and mother-in-law, who had a grandchild on the way. Constance asked when the last scan had taken place, and they described the exact day on which two intriguing things had occurred. One was the dream that Constance had had when Shangdi had appeared before her, which coincided with the passing of Karl's father. All was almost too much for Constance to grasp in one go. She still said nothing of the dream in which the majestic Sea Lord Shangdi reached out for her during her first night in Shanghai.

Karl had arranged to take Orchid to see his parents shortly after the initial part of the funeral, as he believed it was part of his homage to his grandfather to do so. He was naturally eager and somewhat impatient to share the wonderful news with his parents that they were to be grandparents. Knowing that his grandfather had passed away, Karl saw it as the time to herald a new beginning for the family. He mused on the importance of maintaining a balance between the yin and the yang within the family.

He explained to Orchid that, as she was having a child, she should not attend the early part of the funeral. He pointed out that death was viewed as inauspicious, and it is thought inappropriate for pregnant women to participate in the funeral itself. However, after the formalities of the funeral had passed, Orchid would be warmly welcomed, bringing new life to the family group.

Upon arrival at his parents' villa in Shanghai, Karl and Orchid would not wait to share their wonderful news.

They did not have to wait long, for, like Constance, the Kams looked at Orchid, noting how she radiated health and happiness, and were able to make an informed guess. Karl knew that when he shared the news with his parents, their reaction would be a mixture of excitement, joy, and a deep sense of responsibility.

Becoming grandparents is a significant event in Chinese culture, and the news is met with immense happiness. It is the custom for Chinese parents to view the birth of a grandchild as a continuation of the family lineage and a new chapter in their own lives.

Karl took time to explain to Orchid the generosity they could expect from his parents and his extended family, which would come with the expectation that they would all be actively involved in the child's upbringing. This could include financial assistance, practical help with childcare, and possibly offering advice on parenting, including unsolicited advice based on their own experiences and traditional beliefs about raising children. Karl assured Orchid that they would handle this together to avoid tension. He spoke about how a child could strengthen family bonds and, in some way, adjust the roles within the family, particularly in that he would be expected to shoulder more responsibility for the child in a practical sense. Orchid had learnt that the concept of carrying on the family line was something deeply rooted in the aristocratic family she had joined.

Mr. and Mrs. Kam spoke lovingly of their desire to protect Orchid and her child, explaining the custom of the 'sitting month', a thirty-day period of rest for the mother after childbirth. During this time, Mrs. Kam said she would be happy to care for her, preparing particularly nourishing food to help her build up strength following the birth. It had been agreed that the birth would take place in the UK, after which, when safe to do so, Constance, Karl, Orchid, and the new baby would spend time in Shanghai, getting used to having a family of their own. This visit would coincide with the 'one month' celebration of the birth (manyue).

Arrangements for the funeral of the mighty Sea Lord Shangdi were progressing and nearing a conclusion following the selection of an auspicious date for Karl's father's passing. Orchid had witnessed a Chinese almanac (Tung Shing) being consulted to determine a suitable day, with Karl pointing out that everything being done for the funeral was aimed at ensuring a smooth transition to the afterlife for the mighty Shangdi. Shangdi was to be buried in his beautifully embroidered ceremonial robes, befitting his stature and position in the Chinese community.

Among the many gifts created for Shangdi, mostly fashioned from red paper and carefully photographed by Karl, was an exquisite paper replica of the grand Chinese Junk. Reflecting on how for countless years, Shangdi had been its Sea Lord and master, and the model captured the vessel's majesty and the pride of its long and storied history.

Karl took the time to describe the funeral process, including the offerings of food, incense, and joss paper, all made to ensure comfort and prosperity in the afterlife. He also told Orchid that many people had brought white envelopes containing money (bai jin), as white symbolised mourning rather than joy. Knowing the Kam family's prosperity, it was anticipated that the bai jin would be donated to a charity of their choice.

Although saddened not to be able to attend, Orchid nonetheless shared in the funeral's process and progress remaining in the background. Constance had been eagerly awaiting Karl and Orchid's return to the UK, and they brought with them a copy of the formal invitation for her safekeeping. When she opened the envelope, her breath caught. There, in elegant script, was the name 'Shangdi'. For a moment, she could scarcely believe it. Finally, she understood that the mighty Sea Lord she had once encountered aboard the majestic, ornate Chinese Junk, the Shangdu, was indeed her new son-in-law's grandfather. The revelation left her trembling with awe and wonder.

So many memories and thoughts came flooding back, and she resolved to ask her son and daughter how much they remembered of that fateful trip on the mighty Junk from Repulse Bay to Hong Kong's magnificent harbour so many years ago. Constance had felt intense sadness on learning of Shangdi's death. In many ways, she had imagined that hearing such news might help put something longstanding to rest. Instead, she found the opposite: thoughts of Shangdi were now uppermost in her mind. Constance finally admitted to herself that she had always hoped, against hope, that she might meet him again in this life. Perhaps the afterlife would hold that possibility however?

On her return from Shanghai, Orchid looked and felt well. She explained to Constance that upon hearing of her pregnancy, Mrs. Kam had taken it upon herself to care for her and her unborn child with the greatest attention. Orchid said she had been delighted when she saw the suite of rooms the Kams had dedicated to them as a wedding gift. "Tears came to my eyes, mother, when I saw the incredible nursery," she said. She went on to tell her mother that during their time in Shanghai, the Kams had furnished the nursery with many beautiful pieces of Chinese-style furniture, furnishings, and wall coverings, including magnificent dragons. Mrs. Kam had tactfully included Karl and Orchid in the choice of décor and soft furnishings. The photograph Orchid had taken of the furnished nursery showcased the very best of East and West, blending traditional and modern fixtures and fittings.

As her pregnancy progressed, Orchid planned for the birth. She had been overjoyed when told at one of the scans that she was having a little girl and reassured Karl that she had so hoped this would be the case, though she remained, convinced that a son would one day follow to carry on his aristocratic Chinese line. Among the many photographs, including those taken at the funeral, one made Constance catch her breath. It depicted a six-foot tissue-paper replica of the mighty Junk, the Shangdu, its intricate details capturing the grandeur and power of the legendary vessel.

Constance spent several happy months staying with Karl and Orchid, there to help when the wonderful day arrived and she could see her new grandchild. Karl was unsure about being at the birth but was delighted when Constance and Orchid confirmed that they would ensure that the birth would be celebrated in line with traditions practised by both families.

During a lengthy telephone call with Mrs. Kam, Constance learned that naming a child was a significant event to them, often involving careful consideration of the child's future, family heritage and cultural traditions. Names were viewed as far more than just identifiers; they were believed to influence the child's personality, destiny and even their luck. Karl and Orchid agreed that the child would take both their surnames to maintain lineage within both families. The child would also be given a 'milk' name (nickname) to ensure she felt a sense of her own identity in two multi-extended families.

During the many shared phone calls between Constance and Mrs. Kam following the announcement of the pending grandchild, Constance was able to establish Mrs. Kam's milk name. Mr. Kam joined the call, explaining that when he first met his wife's parents, they told him they had named his wife 'Lilly', which meant 'gracious and charming'. He added that every day he had known her, she had lived up to her beautiful milk name. Constance told them that her name meant strength, reliability and perseverance.

Mr. Kam hesitated and thought for a moment as if trying to decide whether he should mention that his father, Shangdi, had told him many years ago of an intriguing woman he had met during the fall of Hong Kong, adding that under different circumstances, his father would have sought to make her his wife. Shangdi had told Karl's father about the strength and determination that he had so admired when he first met her and her two young children, never imagining that their worlds would one day collide in such a way.

The telephone line seemed to go silent. Constance could barely breathe. Mrs. Kam appeared to be staring at her husband, firstly in awe at the lovely comments he had made about her and the story his father had told him many years ago, which he had not shared with her until now.

Constance decided to relate key aspects of her meeting with Shangdi and how he had undoubtedly been instrumental in getting her and her children to safety. She mentioned the beautiful jade that still hung around her neck on a heavy gold chain. At this point, Mrs. Kam commented on how she had noticed the jade during the visit Constance had made to Shanghai, not understanding its significance. They all found it somewhat challenging to pick up the easy conversation they had previously enjoyed, gradually discussing their forthcoming granddaughter. All agreed that they would talk again as soon as the child had been born, and that while the birth was to take place in the UK, Constance, Karl, Orchid, and their grandchild would travel to Shanghai one month after the birth.

A three-way call took place, enabling Karl and Orchid to share their wonderful news with both parents. Their baby girl had been born that morning, and both mother and baby were doing well. All were emotional, very relieved, and excited. Orchid announced that the baby girl would be named Lilly Moon Flower, after both of her grandmothers.

It was a beautiful name for an incredible, delicate and beautiful little girl who, even at this early age, shone with Eastern and Western beauty. After the call, Constance thought of the lovely little child who seemed to encompass everything dear to her. She bore a resemblance to her late husband, her English grandfather, in her features, except for her beautiful almond-shaped eyes and jet-black hair. Born into such a remarkable line of descendants, Constance could hardly wait to see her grow and flourish. Lilly Moon Flower came into the world in the Year of the Rabbit, a year celebrated as the luckiest of all in the Chinese zodiac. It was a joyous beginning for an extraordinary, deeply cherished and long-awaited little girl.

CHAPTER TWENTY-NINE

As promised, Constance, Karl, Orchid and Lilly Moon Flower set off to meet Lilly's Shanghainese grandparents and their extended family. Mr. and Mrs. Kam were seeking to create a wonderland of love and a promise of unending support for their son, daughter-in-law and their much-awaited one-month-old granddaughter.

In Chinese culture, the period immediately following a baby's birth is a time of both rest and celebration, known as "zou yuezi". During this time, the mother recuperates while observing specific traditions and following dietary guidelines designed to support her recovery.

Constance had taken great care of Orchid and the baby on her return home from the hospital. She knew that at the end of the month, a celebration called the "Full Moon Celebration" or "Red Egg and Ginger Party" was being arranged by Karl's parents, timed to coincide with their arrival in Shanghai. The full moon celebration, Constance was advised, was held to mark the baby's survival and to introduce the baby to the extended family and friends. It is also a Chinese tradition rooted in the concept of maintaining balance between yin and yang in the body, with pregnancy considered a yang state and childbirth a yin state that requires rebalancing. Constance was surprised to hear that the complete moon celebration was a symbolic gesture to celebrate the baby's survival at a time when infant mortality rates were historically high in China.

On arrival with their precious baby girl, showing Lilly Moon Flower to her Chinese family was something Karl thought he might never see. He had demonstrated that he had progressed into adulthood through marriage and fatherhood. His parents had invited guests to share in their happiness and to meet the newest member of this auspicious family. Guests brought gifts of money in red envelopes (lai see), wishing the precious little girl good luck and prosperity.

In line with Chinese tradition and its rich culture, the Kams also arranged a banquet for their guests, which included traditional red eggs and pickled ginger. Constance was seen as a guest of honour together with the Kam family, their son and daughter-in-law. Lilly Moon Flower lay in a beautiful, colourful and heavily decorated Chinese cradle. She was wearing a simple Chinese baby robe. The robe, called Baijia Pao, was a patchwork robe made from fabric scraps supplied by one hundred family members. The robe featured a rich array of colours, with red predominating to symbolise prosperity, and was decorated with intricate embroidery depicting auspicious symbols of longevity alongside geometric patterns, including squares, triangles and hexagons.

Orchid and Karl were mesmerised by their daughter and the way in which their unique jewel of a daughter was being revered and welcomed by the family guests who had been invited to meet her and celebrate her arrival into their long ancestral line.

Constance recalled being advised, when first meeting her daughter's future in-laws, not to be surprised by the way Chinese parents openly discussed personal matters such as finances and the future. Mr. Kam was by now aware that Constance knew of his long ancestral lineage and the fact that his father was the mighty Sea Lord Shangdi. The Kams introduced this when other guests had left, leaving just the immediate Kams and Constance. He explained that it was not automatic that he would inherit his father's title of Sea Lord. However, he had been advised that Shangdi had named his first-born son, Mr. Kam, as his designated heir. Traditional Chinese culture considers military strength, political alliances and the ability to maintain control. Should Mr. Kam be found lacking in these attributes, his claim to power would be contested. Shangdi's wishes were to be met, as Mr. Kam was infinitely worthy. As such, he became an acknowledged Sea Lord.

Constance and Orchid were somewhat taken aback and a little concerned about how such an honour would affect their future lives. Mr. Kam, who had known from a very young age that in all probability he would inherit from his father, explained how, over the centuries, the role had changed a great deal. He would inherit his father's lands and possessions in the same way as a son would inherit from his family in the UK. He explained that the title was largely symbolic, a recognition of his standing in the community, and carried no extra responsibility or power. Constance vividly remembered the majesty of the mighty Shangdi during their time aboard his Chinese Junk, reflecting on his grandeur and benevolence as perceived through the eyes of his devoted, respectful Chinese crew.

Saying goodbye to the Kams proved to be extremely difficult, made more so by the distress demonstrated by Mrs. Kam at knowing her new grandchild was heading back to the UK and out of easy reach of her adoring Chinese grandparents. Karl was the first to explain that he, Orchid and the wondrous Lilly Moon Flower would have two homes: the one they had set up together in anticipation of their child's birth, and the other in the wonderful suite of rooms his parents had created for them in the grounds of their fascinating Shanghai villa. They saw no hardship nor difficulty in moving between the two houses, adding that their marriage had truly opened up the world for all of them. "With flights readily available, travel is made easy for us," Karl added.

All agreed that the world had indeed opened up to travel, as Constance pointed out that there would always be a welcome in Wales for all of them. They departed feeling a little less troubled and looking forward to all being able to watch the exquisite Lilly Moon Flower grow up through phone calls and photographs. "We are all going to become frequent flyers," Mrs. Kam added with a weak but meaningful smile on her face as the little group prepared to depart.

The final gesture from Mr. and Mrs. Kam was to bestow a traditional gold Chinese Longevity Lock to their precious granddaughter. Mrs. Kam explained that when given to the first-born grandchild, it symbolises good fortune, health and protection from misfortune. The beautiful gold lock was flat in design, with no moving parts. Karl turned to his parents, bowing deeply to acknowledge that, in that moment; they were symbolically 'locking' their new child's health to the earth, protecting the precious Lilly Moon Flower from any harm. A reverent silence followed such a magnanimous gesture. With tears in their eyes, they embraced and said their au revoir, never goodbye!

CHAPTER THIRTY

After an uneventful homeward-bound flight, Constance arrived home with Karl, Orchid and the wondrous Lilly Moon Flower, and all settled into a routine, keeping in close contact with Mr. and Mrs. Kam.

Constance knew she was very fortunate to live within driving distance of Karl and Orchid's home. She eagerly took many photographs of Lilly for her absent grandparents. They all became 'frequent flyers', making sure that both sets of grandparents saw as much as possible of their beautiful grandchild. They shared in her uniqueness, her beauty, and, in some way, her magic.

Life for Constance was fulfilled in so many ways. In her retirement, she took time to stand and stare and think. As she grew a little older, her thoughts and dreams were sometimes confused, containing visions of her husband and Shangdi, even though both were now dead. Her dreams invariably focused on her time in Hong Kong with her husband at Stanley Fort, where she knew that she had fallen in love with the Chinese and their wondrous culture. She also had the most vivid dreams, all in red and gold, of the majestic junk, the Shangdu, and the mighty Shangdi. She imagined from time to time that Shangdi was attempting to contact her. Not fully understanding the concept of afterlife, she found this unnerving. However, the next time Shangdi appeared before her in her dreams, holding out a silky red ribbon for her to take hold of, she tentatively tried to grasp it but to no avail. He and the ribbon seemed to fade away, leaving her with only a vivid memory. "Perhaps another time?" she thought to herself.

The arrival of a son for Karl and Orchid, two years later, completed their little family. As he grew stronger, many remarked on the firmness of his character and how much he was beginning to resemble his Chinese grandfather.

Both children, with the aid of their adoring grandparents, travelled with apparent ease between East and West, each time seeming to spend longer in Shanghai as Karl's parents grew older.

Lilly Moon Flower demonstrated a wholesome mix of East and West. Her brother, who had been named Karl Jun, meaning 'king, ruler' after his father, leaned more towards the ancient Chinese culture of total focus on family and honouring tradition. At the same time, Karl Jun also embraced many parts of his Western culture. He demonstrated a keenness for understanding Chinese customs, linked to a deep respect for hierarchy and an appreciation for harmony over conflict. Many times, Constance found herself marvelling at her children and grandchildren. They gave her immense satisfaction and pride. She knew her husband would have been proud of the children they had created together. She mused on whether he was in fact looking down on them, experiencing the richness of their current life. Constance certainly hoped so, as her last memory of her husband had been at a time of such sadness and heartache.

Constance found great solace in the closeness and friendship that had developed between herself and Mr. and Mrs. Kam.

She felt very much a part of their extended family and encouraged Orchid to make Karl Jun and Lilly Moon Flower also fully aware of their many relatives still living in and around Londonderry.

Relatives in Northern Ireland had changed over the years, with sadly many of the older generation passing peacefully away and younger aunts, uncles and cousins joining the family. The Kams spent several Christmases with Constance and her Northern Irish extended family, causing Mr. Kam to greatly admire their strength, determination and love of family. He announced that getting to know Constance and her family had shown him how very similar the two large families were. "We may follow different traditions, but in reality we think, feel and do many of the same things."

Constance found it unbelievable how the two families had gelled. Her love and fascination with China and its many traditions, customs, smells and sights had become heightened with every visit she made to Shanghai, and the Kams used similar words when describing their new love and appreciation of all things western.

Life in North Wales continued to provide stimulation for Constance. She felt fortunate to have found such a beautiful Welsh cottage with a mature garden that provided space for a variety of orchids and other exotic plants. She found great satisfaction in tending them, as her neighbours regarded them as rare and unusual and were always fascinated by her stories of the Far East.

Try though she might, she could not grow what would have been an extremely treasured and beautiful Moon Flower. She knew that the origins of the Moon Flower were in Brazil, but that it loved the humid climate offered by most countries in the Far East. However, during one visit to Shanghai, Mrs. Kam, who now agreed to the use of her milk name, Lilly, had obtained a Moon Flower plant and placed it in the shared courtyard of her villa.

To the utmost delight of everyone concerned, but especially Constance, during one of her many visits to Shanghai on a beautiful moonlit night, as she relaxed in the courtyard, a magnificent perfume permeated the night air. Lo and behold, the Moon Flower had opened in all its loveliness.

It was a truly magnificent sight and smell, which brought tears flooding to her eyes. Memories came rushing back. The fleeting beauty and allure of the flower, living for just one day and opening in harmony with the moon on its chosen night, reminded Constance of the depth of feeling and attraction between herself and Shangdi. "Can love be that instantaneous?" she wondered. Like the Moon Flower after which Shangdi had named her, their time together had been brief yet profoundly significant, a single and unforgettable moment in time

She wondered to herself whether, had her husband survived his dreadful time as a prisoner of war in Osaka, she would ever have told him of their meeting. She felt the answer would always have been no, thinking that had her husband lived, Shangdi's impact would surely have been less. Constance brought her thoughts back to the beautiful courtyard and looked around at those present, considering herself oh so very lucky to be surrounded by so many wonderful people and seeing a beautiful Moon Flower in all its magnificence.

CHAPTER THIRTY-ONE

Lilly Moon Flower and her brother Karl Jun were growing up into amazing teenagers. They both had the most beautiful, limpid dark eyes and skin that seemed to glow. Constance thought for a moment about how much their lives had been enriched because of their mixed heritage.

She noticed that their mannerisms were no different from those of their English cousins. However, being of mixed heritage seemed to make them even more comfortable in their own skin, showing high self-esteem. With all the love and support they received, they were already growing into confident, high-achieving individuals with a strong sense of identity and a deep respect for diversity.

Lilly Moon Flower was preparing to follow her mother and father and study at Belfast University, focusing on Chinese cultural beliefs and heritage, something that fascinated her.

CHAPTER THIRTY-TWO

A unique aspect of the ever-growing bond with Mr. and Mrs. Kam included sharing key festivals in each country to further enrich everyone's perspective and understanding.

The Kams were overjoyed when Lilly joined them for an Easter egg hunt in the garden of their lovely villa. In return, Mr. and Mrs. Kam shared details of the Hungry Ghost Festival with Constance, feeling it was especially meaningful following the death of Shangdi, Mr. Kam's father. They explained that on the fifteenth day of the seventh lunar month, it is believed that the gates of the underworld open, allowing the spirits of deceased relatives to once again roam the earth.

They had explained that tradition included burning incense and offering food to appease the wandering spirits and ensure their ancestors were well cared for. This had been thought appropriate; as they firmly believed, the soul of Shangdi may now have left the underworld and be seeking to achieve things he had not been able to do during his time on earth.

Whilst Constance found it all extremely disturbing and confusing at that time, Karl's family were happy at the thought of being able to offer food and drink to ease the majestic Sea Lord's earthly wanderings. Constance was left with so much to think about regarding the glorious and mighty Sea Lord, so she decided to see if they would expand a little more, giving her perhaps an opening to tell them of her time with Shangdi and their meeting on his majestic Chinese Junk, the Shangdu.

Constance felt there could be no better moment to finally unburden herself to her entire family. She spoke of the fear she had felt when she heard that Hong Kong was to fall to the Japanese, and how the military men had been taken into captivity, leaving the women and children to fend for themselves.

She went on to say that, she was aware the British Government was endeavouring to commandeer warships to rescue the women and children. However, time was passing and little or no information was making its way to Constance who, as her husband had been a senior officer, took it upon herself to collate information to keep the other families informed.

She recounted how very kind, very old Chinese men and women had been when meeting them on the beach to see how they could help. She commented on how she had never come across such kindness despite the risk to themselves when, out of the darkness, a Chinese woman bobbing up and down on her home-made sampan had called to them, picking them up on her sampan, zigzagging from the beach out into the deep, murky waters of Hong Kong and the South China Sea.

Constance looked around her and much to her surprise, Orchid spoke up, adding how the Junk had appeared out of nowhere and how the old Chinese lady had helped them to board the mighty Junk. Constance was overjoyed that Orchid could remember so much from so long ago, but Orchid confirmed how she also remembered the sailor with the silver teeth and little bird that foretold them they would live long and be happy.

Constance was consumed with guilt for not encouraging her children to speak about those vivid memories from time to time. Orchid replied that there had been so many adventures, almost too many to talk about.

The moon still shone. The beautiful aroma of the intriguing Moon Flower still wafted, providing an almost magical sensation of scent and otherworldly stimulation. Constance looked around her and realised at that moment that she held them all in the palm of her hand. Never having been in such a situation before, she was unsure as to how to continue. It felt as though enough had been said, except for the beautiful, cool, green jade, which hung around her neck.

Realising she was fingering it whilst she spoke, Mr. Kam asked if the jade still had any significance to what she had just told them. Constance reiterated Shangdi's words when he gave it to her and that she had handed him a red ribbon taken only moments earlier from Orchid's hair.

Orchid reached for her hair, as though imagining the moment was happening again. Those present watched her unusual reaction, sensing that she could almost feel her mother reaching for the ribbon to give to the magnificent Sea Lord she vaguely remembered meeting as a very young girl.

From that moment on, Constance and those present became truly one close family unit with shared values, deep respect, and, most of all, a strong determination to think and be as one family entity. Constance left Shanghai, leaving Orchid, Karl and their two children to continue their holiday.

Arriving back in the UK, Constance felt she had gained some relief in sharing out loud full details of her meeting with Shangdi. She felt that those present understood how magical and significant the moment had been, and how the entire experience aboard the Chinese junk had profoundly influenced Constance and her children throughout their lives, and continued to do so still and would for ever more

How time passes oh so very quickly, thought Constance, when receiving a telephone call from Lilly Moon Flower advising her grandmother of her decision to spend a year out from University with her Chinese family in Shanghai and then to go travelling around the Far East, visiting many of the magical places that her grandmother had told her about. It was a wonderous time for Constance knowing that her treasured, beautiful granddaughter was in many ways following in her footsteps.

During her travels, Lilly travelled to many countries around the world, focusing mainly on the wonderous Far East. It was clear that she had inherited her grandmother's deep passion for the region and all that it represented.

Karl Jun was well established in the law firm owned by his father in Shanghai, where Karl and Orchid had moved some ten years earlier, setting up home on the plot of land close to their Chinese grandparents' extensive villa. Constance missed having so much easy access to her children. However, she acknowledged and appreciated the easy access she had had when they were young and growing up and the 'red ribbon' always kept them close.

Fortunately, the young couple also maintained a home in the UK, ensuring that their children would understand and love the rich culture of both societies. Constance saw this as an important factor in their development in a mixed marriage. Frequently, she would reflect on the many times she had journeyed to the Far East from the very first time when embarking on the six-week sea journey to Hong Kong to join her husband. So much water had gone under the bridge since the time when travelling to the other side of the world was looked upon as a mammoth task. For her, it had been a true journey of discovery, opening her mind to the fascination of the Far East and its wonderful culture.

How she loved all her time spent in the eastern hemisphere. The experiences had changed her forever and so long ago, almost without her knowing it, and had produced a daughter who shared her enthusiasm after marrying into the wonderful Kam family from Shanghai. How could that have happened? She mused thinking that had she planned for one of her children to be joined in marriage to a family such as the Kams, she simply could not have done it.

Yet now she had two beautiful mixed-heritage children who had strengthened her bond with China in such a meaningful way. She reflected that if she were ever to have a granddaughter, she would want her to be named Moon Flower, as a reminder of her meeting with the mighty Shangdi, and in her life time she had miraculously achieved that.

CHAPTER THIRTY-THREE

Much to the surprise of Constance, she received a notification from the Ministry of Defence advising her that, unbelievably, some of her original Hong Kong belongings had, after fifty years, been traced.

Constance could hardly believe it and wondered what could possibly be so important. She had never imagined that any of their belongings left behind in Hong Kong, when she and her children had hastily departed, would ever find their way home and back to her.

She felt quite excited to see what was contained in what the military called the MFO, Movements Forwarding Office. Constance could only imagine that her husband had managed to get a small amount of their belongings packed and dispatched before being taken prisoner. What a heartbreaking task that must have been for her husband, Constance thought, having to abandon memories of their short time together, just hoping against hope that they would all eventually be reunited.

With bated breath, Constance waited to hear when the MFO was due for delivery. Suffering from uncertainty and apprehension, on the day of delivery a huge wooden crate arrived. She looked with wonderment at how well preserved the small amount of MFO was, wondering to herself which route it had taken and where it had been before finally arriving in North Wales. She also thought of how very, very difficult it must have been for her husband to quickly gather things that both he and his wife would view as important and meaningful to both of them in later life.

On opening the crate, Constance was mesmerised to see that it contained one item only, and that was the glorious camphor-lined rosewood chest they had bought when she and the children had first arrived in Hong Kong. She opened the chest and was knocked back by the wonderful smell that teased at her senses, bringing her husband and their short time together in Stanley Fort flooding back to her.

How wonderful that an unknown person working in an office within the Military Forwarding Organisation saw delivery of the chest as of the utmost importance and took such care to ensure that it arrived safely. Constance thought to herself how utterly wonderful it was to see the rosewood chest now sitting in her cottage in Wales.

The chest itself, even before searching eagerly through the contents, reminded Constance of how they had laughed when she and her husband decided to purchase such an expensive item. It was a common topic within the military family community in the Far East that you either purchased a rosewood chest or had a new baby! Whilst believing themselves to be realists, not known to believe rumours, they still went ahead and bought the chest, and it was now standing in front of her. "Just in case," her husband had said with a twinkle in his eyes.

When visiting the Chinese craftsman who made the rosewood chest, he had told them in broken English that rosewood chests used a rosewood specifically as it was native to China, pointing out the species known as Dalbergia, a giant slow-growing tree known for its fragrance. He went on to tell them that rosewood chests were used in the eighteenth and nineteenth centuries for transporting tea, silk, and other valuables to Europe. The chests, he went on to say, were always lined with camphor wood, which had an inbuilt insect repellent and had open pores that helped it absorb the potentially damaging moisture.

"You smell, Missy, master?" the Chinese craftsman asked them, holding a piece of camphor wood under their noses!

Constance and her husband felt they had both a geography and a history lesson from the wizened Chinese man, all delivered in his broken English. Having what the craftsman saw as a captive audience and a potential sale coming his way, he pointed out that rosewood chests were traditionally also used for a trousseau, keeping the contents in good order even though they may have travelled by ship through the South China Sea, the Indian Ocean, before traversing the Suez Canal and finally into the Mediterranean.

Coming back to earth in her beautiful Welsh stone cottage, Constance felt herself momentarily immersed in memories, helping her to understand that she had forgotten so much of the rich tapestry of her time with her husband in Hong Kong. It felt good to bring it flooding back. And she let it momentarily engulf her!

She felt both joy and sadness as her mind, heart, and soul seemed to momentarily return to Hong Kong. She opened the beautifully carved rosewood chest with its delicately fashioned brass handles and locks. Unsure where to begin, she lifted out a finely embroidered piece of silk, so smooth and soft to the touch that she could not resist pressing it gently against her face. She could remember the exact stall on the exact market where she bought it musing on whether it was in fact a cousin of Hoi Fung who had handed it to her.

It smelt of everything she remembered, but most of all the cool camphor smell hit her senses. Constance placed the delicate fabric to one side, reaching for items of the children's clothing from when they were very young. She asked herself why she would hold onto items such as this, but realised that many of the items she was about to reveal would have been hastily packed by her husband after she had left their accommodation to get herself and her children to safety away from Hong Kong.

Constance was unaware that military personnel were allowed one visit back to their military accommodation by the Japanese soldiers who were in the process of taking them prisoner, in order to collect a small number of necessities.

Reflecting on what her husband had had to cope with, Constance could only imagine how truly dreadful it must have been to know that the only way he could save his wife and children was to let them make their way out of the Colony of Hong Kong in any way they could. She could not bear to let thoughts such as these creep into her head, as they only brought heartbreak. Constance knew at the time of escaping from the Japanese Imperial Army that it was vital to simply get away, as fast as she could.

With feelings of trepidation, Constance delved deeper to see what she would find in the chest. Something that caught her attention was a large envelope written in her late husband's handwriting. She opened it, noting that it contained a sealed envelope addressed to her and her children. Constance's husband had taken time to write them a letter, knowing there was a good chance that he may never see them again but wanting them to know that he loved them with all his heart and would until the day he died. In the letter, he thanked Constance for being the wife that every man would wish to have, to hold and to love. He begged his children to never forget him, saying they must always remember how very special they are and to remain close to their devoted mother.

Inside the letter was her husband's simple gold wedding band. Constance placed it on her finger, remembering how the two matched in their simplicity and loveliness. This brought memories of their wedding day flooding back. In her memory, the sun shone, she looked elegantly lovely in her white silk wedding gown, and her husband had looked so very handsome in his military dress uniform, complete with sword, George boots, and spurs. How very proud she had been and how fortunate she was to have met and married such a strong, kind, wonderful man.

The letter brought her back to earth with a jolt. The emotion was so strong that, for a moment, Constance felt her husband's presence beside her. She held the letter tightly, his ring glinting on her finger. Leaning back in her chair, lost in thought, she vowed that the next time she saw her children, she would let them read their father's letter.

Also contained in the chest was a letter written in the most beautiful, flourishing handwriting from Constance's husband to his brother-in-law, who was serving in Singapore at the time. The letter was written on fine airmail tissue paper and told of loneliness as Christmas approached. It mentioned being in receipt of a Red Cross food parcel, which had lifted their spirits somewhat. It mentioned how receipt of mail was limited and how they all lived in the hope that tomorrow would bring some news of loved ones. Reading the letter for the first time made Constance realise that her husband had never been able to post the letter, but it seemed he had wanted his brother-in-law to know that he had been thinking of him, thus putting the unread letter in the rosewood chest.

Still holding the letter and seeing her husband's writing, she recalled hearing that the Japanese had used captured prisoners of war in Singapore and used them to help build the Burma-Thailand railway. Thousands had died during the building of the railway, designed to help the Japanese get supplies to their troops overland, as going by sea was costly in terms of manpower and shipping losses. Constance's brother-in-law, she was to learn later, had actually escaped and, with a small group of fellow prisoners, walked long distances across mountainous terrain, facing disease and exhaustion to reach final safety in India and eventually make their way back home to the UK.

From the date on the letter, Constance knew it had been written just before the Japanese invaded Burma. However, reading it gave Constance a greater understanding of the time her husband spent before being taken prisoner. In the letter, he wrote about having a Sunday roast for his Christmas dinner with his friends and how he was missing contact with home, adding that mail deliveries and methods were somewhat haphazard.

Further searches of the rosewood chest revealed photographs of the children with Hoi Fung, the Black and White Chinese amah who had cared for them so devotedly during their two magical years as a family in Hong Kong. They also showed how she had kindly taken in their pets, giving them a home with her own family when the little family had been forced to flee.

Searching further into the chest, Constance found a vintage Chinese umbrella, noting that Mr. Kam had used such an umbrella to offer protection to Orchid on her wedding day. The fascinating umbrella was made of oil paper. Constance recalled when she bought two of these beautiful, colourful umbrellas, being told that the Chinese are thought to have created the first waterproof umbrella and that it had existed for over three thousand years. She had been keen to learn that originally, the umbrellas were made of silk with bamboo frames. In many countries, it is believed that umbrellas are rich in symbolism and superstition. Constance vividly recalled how she had witnessed a team of wonderfully elegant Chinese ladies carry out a never-to-be-forgotten performance featuring the most colourful and beautiful umbrellas, twirling red umbrellas to usher in prosperity.

The next finding was an incredibly colourful tissue paper Chinese Dragon kite. She remembered flying it on the very beach in Repulse Bay with her husband. Once again, she recalled that this had in fact been the very beach from which they had hastily departed from Hong Kong, and where

Constance and her children had first seen the magnificent Junk, the Shangdu. "Things go round and round!" Constance thought.

At that time of flying the kite, Constance had been joined on the beach by a group of young Chinese children, who joined in and flew the magnificent kite. The children told Constance's fascinated children that many people believed that flying a Chinese dragon kite kept evil spirits away, excitedly, adding that flying a dragon kite was a true sign of strength.

An item that Constance found buried deep in the chest was a piece of old wood containing the name 'Kariba' engraved on a small brass plate. Constance and her family had had many happy hours on board The Kariba, a heavy wooden lifeboat taken from a Japanese ship, which Constance and her husband had purchased for themselves. The converted Kariba provided an interesting and extremely unusual space for evening supper parties and lunch parties, an invitation to which was prized by many of their friends. Constance recalled so many happy memories of time spent on the Kariba when, in her memory, the weather was always beautiful, friends were engaging, and everyone always had a tremendous time.

She recalled the day the Kariba lifeboat was wrecked during a massive typhoon, Typhoon Ellen, which had swept up most of the boats moored off the southern coast of the island and dashed them against the rocks after they had broken anchor in the heavy seas that Hong Kong experienced several times each year during the typhoon season

Some little comfort was gained by Constance and her family when told by the harbour master that the Kariba was the last boat to be wrecked and dashed to pieces on the jagged rocks.

Constance found a prominent place for her beautiful rosewood chest of memories, waiting for the next visit of her children to give them the pleasure of viewing its memorable contents.

CHAPTER THIRTY-FOUR

Constance's children and grandchildren were busy but remained in good health and appeared extremely happy.

Lilly Moon Flower, Constance's first Eurasian grandchild, was living up to her name. Many admired her beauty and captivating charm. Her brother, Karl Jun, was growing into a fine young man, following in his father's and grandfather's footsteps by taking on both English and Chinese law cases. Orchid and Karl were visibly proud of their children, feeling blessed that they carried the best qualities of all their grandparents.

On many occasions, Constance found herself reflecting on how very, very lucky she was. One event she brought to mind was a particular gathering in Shanghai of both families, including Lilly Moon Flower and Karl Jun. This was arranged to coincide with the Spring Festival, otherwise known as Chinese New Year. Chinese New Year always brought great entertainment and enjoyment, as it was seen as an event of pure celebration. Lilly Moon Flower never ceased to enjoy seeing the Dragon Dance, watching one wonderful and noisy event carried out by a team of colourfully dressed male and female dancers who hid under a long dragon cloak made of soft rubber and a series of cleverly placed hoops. One member beat the drum as loudly as possible, which made the dragon dance faster, twisting and turning, bringing blessings and warding off evil spirits.

The Kams had kindly hosted the latest Chinese New Year celebration that Constance attended with her children and grandchildren.

Children and grandchildren moved smoothly between their homes in the UK and Shanghai. A truly cosmopolitan family. The feast they shared was exceptional, leaving Constance with the feeling that the Kams saw this as possibly the last time they would all spend together. Age was making travel a little more difficult. She said her farewells to Karl's parents, reflecting on the time they had shared together when everyone had found out that the two families were in so many ways intrinsically linked through the power held by the mighty Sea Lord, Shangdi, and how, by a stroke of luck and hap-chance, their lives had changed forever.

Constance knew that, in the fullness of time, her daughter Orchid's husband would inherit this title and the customs that went with the title of Ancient Sea Lord. She felt her dragon awakening and the embrace of the silken red ribbon they all believed held them close. This gave her some solace in leaving Shanghai for what would probably be the final time, thus possibly severing her connection to Shangdi forever. Whilst in the Far East, she always felt close to him, never feeling able to accept that they would never meet again. Constance had learnt so much from her daughter's in-laws over the years that she shared their belief in the ability to feel and, in some way, communicate with their ancestors. She knew that honouring ancestors was a way of ensuring their blessings. When Constance was in Shanghai over the many years, she had been delighted to visit the beautiful villa, and she understood that familial piety was an attitude of total respect for one's parents and ancestors, one that, in many ways, she could subscribe to. During her life, she had felt the support of her extended family and reflected on how small the difference between her culture and that of the Kams in reality was.

Lilly Moon Flower was turning into an exceptional scholar. Her love and passion for understanding how East and West co-exist in harmony was used as her dissertation, calling on real-life research gained from her English and Chinese grandparents. During a visit to spend time with her grandmother in Wales, Lilly told Constance that she was going to follow in her footsteps and visit many of the places she and her mother had visited throughout their lifetime. Constance noticed how Lilly's beautiful, soft face came to life when talking about her plans. She was amazed at her beauty. Lilly had inherited many of the traits of her Shanghainese female relatives. These included her luxurious, long black hair, straight and wonderfully silky, her dusky, slightly almond-shaped eyes, and her slender figure. During their discussion before she set off on her travels, they agreed that Lilly would send her grandmother postcards, believing this would refresh memories.

Constance smiled to herself as Lilly shared her plans for the future, her memories as vivid as ever. Looking at her lovely granddaughter always brought a flood of recollections. In Lilly Moon Flower, she saw a living connection to the majestic Sea Lord Shangdi, for they shared a great/granddaughter. The thought filled her with joy and deepened her fascination and affection for her beautiful Eurasian grandchild.

Lilly was living up to her heritage, spending time with both sets of her much-loved grandparents. Constance felt so very close to her precious granddaughter, so much so that, as the end of Constance's natural life was moving closer, Lilly was frequently in her grandmother's thoughts. Rather than waiting for Lilly to plan her next visit, as her focus was on planning her trip around the Eastern hemisphere, Constance decided to invite her to spend a very special weekend with her in her beautiful stone cottage in Wales. Lilly was delighted, as she loved every minute she spent in Wales. She loved that Constance always found interesting stories to tell her, which she saw as an essential part of Lilly's multi-cultural heritage.

Lilly was delighted to be visiting the beautiful Welsh cottage. She loved to see how it encompassed the East versus West décor of her studio room, specifically created for her by her grandmother. Her studios truly reflected her Eurasian heritage, of which she was tremendously proud. Lilly had filled her room with so much memorabilia from both of her families and loved to reflect on the inner strength of her English grandmother and the stories she would tell. She was particularly fascinated when Constance talked about how she had to get on the back of her dragon when escaping from Hong Kong with her mother and uncle, getting herself and her children out of the path of the Japanese Army to safety and away from Hong Kong. Constance had told Lilly so many tales, some amusing, some scary, and others at times simply unbelievable, yet so true.

As usual, Constance prepared for Lilly's forthcoming visit, having resolved to explain in greater detail the time spent on the wondrous Chinese junk and her meeting with the most magical Sea Lord, Shangdi, who, through the intervention of fate, turned out to be Lilly's great-grandfather. Constance also wished to let Lilly know that, when she eventually passed from this life, she would like Lilly to inherit the cool, exceptionally beautiful, and, to Constance, oh so precious, green jade that had been given to her many years ago by Shangdi.

She also wished to ask Lilly for a favour, something that had lingered in her thoughts for many years. It was connected to Lilly's grandfather, who had died in a prisoner of war camp in Osaka, Japan, just one week before the war ended in 1945.

After Lilly's arrival and an excellent afternoon tea out on the lawn, Constance began to talk to Lilly, explaining that she, Lilly Moon Flower, is the one actual link between herself and the Sea Lord, Shangdi. She explained in detail the leap that had taken place from when she first met Shangdi and, finding out years later, that her beautiful mixed-race child would, through an unbelievable leap of fate, turn out to also be Shangdi's Eurasian great-grandchild.

Constance felt such raw yet sweet emotion thinking of the two men in her life. One she truly loved and married; the other with whom she shared an out-of-this-world experience. Constance needed Lilly Moon Flower to understand the raw emotion she felt when Shangdi asked Constance to accept a gift from him.

Constance felt calm, yet she could not hide the depth of her emotions as she spoke to Lilly. Feeling so in tune with her grandmother, Lilly sensed that this was a very special moment between them. She looked at Constance with awe and total admiration.

Lilly sat enthralled as her grandmother began her tale. On that day, she saw something different in her grandmother. It was as if Constance were seeing the past with perfect clarity. She spoke of her escape from Hong Kong and the part that Shangdi had played in it, how he had silently watched her, judging her to be special, intense, family-focused, and honest. Constance told of the moment Shangdi spoke to her, explaining the reason why he had chosen the name Moon Flower for her. He found her alluring, hypnotic, steadfast, strong, and above all, a fellow dragon with the ability to communicate on many levels and reach incredible understanding with those she would meet throughout her lifetime.

Constance then expanded on the origin of Lilly Moon Flower's exquisite and meaningful name. Lilly knew that her grandmother in Shanghai had the same milk name as her, 'Lilly'. Constance told Lilly that since meeting Shangdi, she had always prayed for a granddaughter to whom she could lovingly pass the name he had given her to. She said that having such a beautiful Eurasian child, the mix of two powerful, kind, and gentle families, was a truly wondrous event in her lifetime. She added that being able to pass the mystical name Moon Flower to her, while also including the milk name of her Shanghainese grandmother, was a magical event she had never imagined would happen.

Constance told Lilly there was something else she wished to say. She held the cool, beautiful green jade stone in her hand and passed it to Lilly, to hold for a moment. Lilly reached out, gently grasping the stone. It felt calm and smooth, somewhat 'alive', carrying the warmth of her grandmother's hand. She also understood that her great-grandfather, the mighty Sea Lord Shangdi, whom she had never met, had once held it before taking the step that would eventually link two families, bringing East and West together in one extraordinary child. Lilly Moon Flower! What a truly wonderful event.

Lilly was totally overcome. She could not speak for a moment and sat in companionable silence, simply holding her grandmother's frail hand in her own beautiful, pale, delicate one.

After a short time, Constance spoke again, saying that there was something else of great importance she would like Lilly to do. Lilly immediately said, "Anything, Grandmother, just ask." Constance gently reminded her of the Japanese Imperial Army's invasion of Hong Kong and how, when captured, Lilly's English grandfather had been taken prisoner and died just one week before the war ended.

Constance explained that, on her way back to the UK, having been evacuated first to the Philippines and then to Australia, she had received a letter from the War Office in London. She showed Lilly the yellowed-with-age letter, which confirmed that her grandfather had died in a Prisoner-of-War camp in Osaka and had been buried in a British Commonwealth War Cemetery there. Constance said that she had always hoped to visit the grave and pay her respects, expressing her gratitude, but this had not been possible. The enormous task she was asking of Lilly Moon Flower was to undertake this very important duty on grandmother's behalf.

Constance then picked up a letter from a Japanese priest who had taken it upon himself to enshrine the ashes of prisoners of war in his temple in Japan. Lilly held the letter, reading it slowly, grasping the full significance of the compassionate act by a man who had reached out to the families of those who perished in the terrible conflict, spending their final years in captivity, far from the loved ones who mourned them.

The letter was from a Buddhist priest, Shinkai Yamaguchi, who asked if he might take the liberty of writing to families who had lost husbands, brothers, or fathers in the Osaka camps. Lilly read on as the priest explained that he held the ashes of 1,000 souls in his Juganji temple in Osaka. The letter was written in 1958. Shinkai wrote that it was the Buddhist custom to cremate the dead and keep the ashes in the temple for four weeks before burying them in sacred ground. He had done this even for those who had died years earlier.

Lilly Moon Flower read on and learnt that this single Buddhist priest had seen it as an honour to protect the ashes. He had prayed for the souls at his temple every day for decades and would continue to do so until his own passing.

Lilly was speechless, entirely without words, having read such an emotionally charged letter written by someone who had carried out such a compassionate service in recognition of a truly tragic loss. In closing, Shinkai asked the reader to say a silent prayer in memory of the dead and to pray that such a war might never occur again.

In that moment, Lilly and Constance joined in a silent prayer with Shinkai. Lilly resolved there and then to take a one-year sabbatical and travel to Japan, promising to visit her grandfather's grave on behalf of her grandmother. She was deeply moved by what her grandmother had shared and by Shinkai's letter. Sweet tears ran down her face as she felt the weight of her grandmother's commitment and the profound importance of the task entrusted to her.

Being Eurasian, half English and half Chinese, Lilly understood the importance of ancestors who had passed into the afterlife and how, in some way, they influenced the good fortune, or jos, of those still living. In that moment, her grandmother's story resonated deeply. She felt spell-bound, intensely connected to her grandmother and in some ways, to her great-grandfather Shangdi.

Constance felt a quiet sense of relief after the time spent with her granddaughter, silently hoping that Lilly Moon Flower's visit to the Juganji temple would take place before she passed from this life.

The farewell was tender and emotional. Both Lilly and Constance felt bound together by their shared experience, exhausted yet fulfilled by the intensity of their time together. Lilly knew she had many plans to make and responsibilities to fulfil, in order to carry out her grandmother's wishes exactly as promised.

CHAPTER THIRTY-FIVE

Lilly lost no time in explaining to Orchid and Karl, her mother and father, her intention to spend one year out from university in Belfast on a sabbatical in Japan whilst visiting her grandfather's grave in Osaka. She told her parents of the deeply moving discussions she had had with her grandmother and how Constance intended to bequeath the beautiful jade stone to her as a symbol of their joint families' heritage. They offered their full support.

Lilly thought through how best she could take this meaningful journey entirely on her own, seeking to achieve so much. She looked at what would be the easiest route for her. She quickly found out that regular flights went from Shanghai to Japan and that the flight was a mere three hours. Her plan, therefore, was to spend a little time with her grandparents in Shanghai and fly to Japan from there.

Lilly found that with every visit to Shanghai, she was always surprised at how quickly she stepped into her Chinese 'self'. It helped that, with the help of her Chinese grandmother, she had the most wondrous range of colourfully decorated Cheongsams hanging in her closet in Shanghai. With this in mind, she quickly established that she could fly quite light from the UK as most of the clothes she had in her wardrobe in Shanghai would be eminently suitable to wear in Japan.

Bustling with excitement at taking a year out to see more of the Far East and allowing her Chinese 'self' to expand, Lilly looked forward to understanding new customs and, most importantly, to meeting the Buddhist priest Shinkai who had kindly written to her grandmother. If not Shinkai, then perhaps one of his relatives at the Juganji temple in Osaka.

Lilly felt privileged to have been asked by her grandmother to take on such an important task. She felt very much up to it and wondered if it was her own dragon that was stirring and coming to life? She knew that after her last visit to see her grandmother, she had felt different, believing that she could achieve so much more than she had ever imagined.

Lilly had inherited her grandmother's keen sense of research before making any major decision, so she began exploring universities in Japan that offered a one-year study programme focusing on the nation's history, beliefs, and cultural traditions.

However, top of Lilly's list was to identify the best way of saying thank you to the relatives of the Buddhist priest who had taken it upon himself to look after and honour the ashes of so many prisoners of war who had died in Japan.

Lilly applied and was accepted into a one-year postgraduate programme at Osaka University. The programme was to be taught primarily in English, with Japanese offered as a secondary language. The University of Osaka was chosen as her place of formal study for several reasons, one of which was its proximity to the Buddhist temple where her grandfather was buried. Upon further research, Lilly was delighted to discover that Osaka was in fact one of Japan's top public universities.

Lilly Moon Flower realised that while her English family and her Chinese family were avid globe-trotters, she would be the first from either family to visit Japan. Lilly looked forward to her year away with trepidation, tempered with a great deal of excitement.

There was much for Lilly to learn about Japan and its unique culture. When in Shanghai with her Chinese grandparents, they told her of the vast changes that Japan had faced at the end of World War II. They described how it had undergone a significant transformation during the Allied occupation, led primarily by the Americans, who guided the Japanese into a period of demilitarisation, the establishment of a democratically elected government, and a significant focus on economic recovery.

They went on to explain that the occupation of Japan had brought about sweeping social and political reforms, including the establishment of a new constitution and the redistribution of land. Everyone was aware that the Japan Lilly would be visiting was now regarded as a global economic power, maintaining strong ties with the United States of America.

CHAPTER THIRTY-SIX

The flight from Shanghai to Osaka was swift and sure, compared to the lengthy journeys her grandmother, Constance, had made many years ago, taking her two young children with her. A frequent flyer in every sense, Lilly travelled back and forth between the UK and Shanghai. Spending time in her wonderful studio bedrooms, she felt privileged and incredibly lucky.

On arrival in Japan, Lilly was delighted to find that Osaka was a bustling metropolis with a rich history and a vibrant presence. The city, a fellow traveller told her, was known for its commercial prowess and unique dialects, and was experiencing the start of the new decade with a mix of optimism and challenge. Perhaps just the right time to come, thought Lilly Moon Flower with much optimism?

Fellow students at the University of Osaka shared their knowledge and observations with Lilly, telling her that the country was renowned for its unique blend of the past and the present. Lilly loved its rich cultural heritage, distinctive cuisine, and breathtaking natural landscapes, eagerly soaking up what she was seeing, feeling and hearing. She fell in love with Japan immediately.

Coming from a family that deeply believed in the power and strength of internal dragons, Lilly was delighted to discover that dragons in Japan were also seen as powerful beings with a long and rich history. She learnt that Japanese dragons were often depicted as benevolent, serpentine creatures associated with wisdom, water, and protection.

Lilly Moon Flower knew that Constance would be keen to learn of such things. She was fascinated by this and immediately sent her grandmother in Wales a postcard showing a wonderful, magical dragon, knowing this would bring a host of memories flooding back to her. The picture on the postcard was of an extremely prominent eight-headed dragon known as King of the Seas. Being naturally inquisitive, Lilly asked why the dragon seemed to be so important to the Japanese people. She was told that in their traditional beliefs, dragons were related to the ancestors of the first Emperor of Japan, therefore holding significant importance as a symbol of the emperor.

She found that the style of long and short lectures delivered at Osaka University, supported by interactive seminars with increased emphasis on research and presentations, was a model that Lilly found particularly helpful.

Whilst believing that she could get by in terms of her course material and tuition, some fluency in Japanese seemed somewhat essential for daily life. Initially, Lilly struggled when accessing information and building relationships with peers and faculty. However, being realistic, she knew it would take time, time that she felt she had and was willing to use to squeeze every morsel of information, knowledge, cultural understanding, and opportunity out of this beautiful country.

Lilly found the overall educational system rather formal but felt pleased at this straightforward method of learning, and by a stroke of luck, seemed to suit her learning style quite well.

As time went on, Lilly realised that although her skills were improving, she still struggled with formal communication. She began to feel that a cultural shift was needed if she was to get the most out of her studies. Misunderstandings still arose between her and some of the Japanese lecturers, but both sides recognised that these stemmed from cultural differences, differences that would eventually be overcome with greater understanding.

What Lilly found the hardest was feeling that she did not quite belong, which to her was crucial for academic success and, most importantly, for her overall well-being.

International students with whom Lilly frequently spoke commented on how high the living costs were. However, Lilly knew she was in a privileged position, as she was supported financially and, most importantly, emotionally by both parents and indeed grandparents, who fully understood her reasons for spending a year in Japan.

Lilly found that one good aspect of studying in Osaka was the public transport, which was efficient, reliable, and relatively inexpensive. This allowed some of her friends to take part-time jobs to ease their finances. Lilly thought that she would do the same, as it would help her colloquial Japanese. She desperately wanted to become more involved with her fellow students, so she tried harder to embrace both the academic and cultural aspects of Japanese life, engaging more deeply with the local culture.

CHAPTER THIRTY-SEVEN

After three months in Japan, Lilly was feeling a little homesick, and her grandmother sensed this. Even though Lilly had been brought up to enjoy her own company, she was elated when she received a telephone call from Constance, saying she was in Shanghai with the Kams and wished to send her an air ticket to Shanghai, giving her the chance to join them during her short exeat. Lilly eagerly agreed.

On arrival in Shanghai, she flew into the arms of her grandmother, Constance, first sensing her eagerness to hear about her time in Osaka, and then, with a little more decorum, embraced her Shanghainese grandparents. Everybody felt a little emotional, for a variety of personal reasons. All knew that Lilly living her life in Japan brought mixed memories. Constance's memories were linked to Lilly being in the country that had caused such major upheaval to her life and had taken away her wonderful husband. The Kams, whilst never having been to Japan, were aware of how the Japanese Imperial Army had acted when invading their own beautiful country on its way to capturing Burma.

Being in her studio room in her grandparents' truly magical villa, Lilly felt once more at home. The Kams were, as always, superb hosts, providing every opportunity for Lilly to whisper to Constance about her plans to find the Juganji Temple to visit her grandfather's grave, and for Lilly to tell them of any issues that she was finding difficult.

Lilly was mesmerised by the small grove of Chinese Orange Trees that had grown beautifully since her last visit to Shanghai. These were in the central, open, shared courtyard of the villa. The perfume was heady and seemed to fill every space with such a sweet fragrance. Constance told Lilly that the trees were originally from a Chinese Orange sapling given to her by a sailor onboard the Shangdu, and how Constance herself now had a fine Chinese Orange citrus tree growing in her garden in Wales

CHAPTER THIRTY-EIGHT

After spending time with her grandparents, Lilly felt more content and at peace with how her life was progressing. She decided to arrange a visit to the Juganji Buddhist Temple, which she had learnt was built in the 1500s and was one of the oldest temples in Japan. It was situated halfway up Mount Ikoma and was said to offer a panoramic view of the City of Osaka.

Having learned of Lilly's planned visit to the temple, several of her friends showed a keen interest, explaining a little more about the temple and saying that the reason it was situated halfway up the mountain was to provide a sense of isolation and tranquillity, both ideal for meditation and other religious practices.

Lilly listened with interest and curiosity, realising that she was beginning to feel a little bit Japanese herself. Her fellow students found her intriguing and very beautiful, and began to feel accepted. This was confirmed when she received several invitations to visit her classmates' homes and meet their families, something she recognised as both an honour and a privilege.

Two of her fellow students said they would like to join her when she visited the temple. Being sensitive and understanding the reasons for Lilly's visit, they were cautious in their request. However, Lilly was more than willing, as she was happy to share this momentous occasion with them and knew their ability to speak Japanese would help smooth out any possible barriers and avoid embarrassment, something Lilly was very aware of.

Lilly planned the visit to ensure that she was respectful of the sacred space she was visiting. On arrival, she removed her shoes and replaced them with the sweet, delicate little soft slippers provided for visitors. She had dressed modestly and ensured she and her fellow visitors refrained from making loud noises. Above all, Lilly wished to ensure that before leaving the temple, she had the chance, if it was allowed, to take some discreet but meaningful photographs to share with her grandmother in Wales.

As Lilly and her friends tentatively made their way into the temple following the designated pathways, the little group was delighted when a priest, dressed in fine embroidered robes, approached them. Bowing gently to Lilly and her friends, who all respectfully returned the bow, he asked if this was their first visit and why they had chosen to visit his wonderful, tranquil temple.

Lilly Moon Flower bowed and introduced herself to the Buddhist priest, who returned her bow and introduced himself as Chief Priest Yamaguchi of the Juganji Temple. Something about the Chief Priest's name seemed familiar to Lilly as she explained the purpose of her visit, saying that her two Japanese friends had come to give her a little support, as they too had never had the opportunity to visit such a wonderful place.

The priest was fascinated to hear why Lilly had made such a long journey on behalf of her grandmother. He was visibly moved and asked the little group to follow him to where the ashes of more than 1,000 men of different nationalities who had died in camps in Japan were enshrined.

Lilly and her friends silently and somewhat reverently followed Chief Priest Yamaguchi. They shared an 'under the eyes' glance between themselves, feeling a little uncertain. Yamaguchi led them to the most beautifully maintained green pasture, dotted with simple, discrete headstones bearing the names of those who had died while detained in Japanese Prisoner-of-War camps during the war.

Lilly's friends stepped back as she knelt in front of one of the small marble headstones. The graves were arranged alphabetically, so the grave of her grandfather, beginning with a 'B', was among the first they came to. After a moment or two, Yamaguchi gently took Lilly's small hand and helped her to her feet, bowing his head as he said a prayer for the departed soul of her grandfather. Lilly's friends looked on in awe.

Everyone had tears running down their cheeks; it was a sad, yet beautiful moment. Lilly's thoughts turned to her grandmother in Wales, feeling relieved that she had carried out her wishes. She asked if she could take a photograph to show her grandmother when she returned home.

Yamaguchi said that while taking photographs was discouraged, he would allow her to take a photo of her grandfather's grave, especially for Lilly's highly respected grandmother. Family and ancestor worship were essential facets of Japanese culture.

Lilly's friends felt that they should leave her alone with the priest for such a sacred moment. They bid him farewell, bowing low to Yamaguchi and thanking him sincerely. As they left the temple, mindful of the expectations of visitors, each of them made a small donation to support the temple's upkeep and continued operation.

Lilly was still standing, gazing at the beautifully maintained field of graves, thinking how peaceful and tranquil it felt, and somehow absorbing that feeling into her body. She vowed to transfer that feeling to her grandmother when she returned to the UK. She explained how she was feeling to Yamaguchi and looking at him, Lilly could tell that he knew precisely how moved she had been. The priest thought to himself how unusual it was for such a young woman to show such strength and harmony, signs that he so admired.

Lilly was on the verge of leaving when Chief Priest Yamaguchi turned to her and asked if he could be presumptive and request that she kindly join him in a Japanese Tea Ceremony in honour of all those who had fallen during the Second World War. Lilly was taken aback but felt compelled to agree, having heard that the Tea Ceremony was viewed as extremely sacred, which seemed eminently appropriate at that time. She felt not quite herself and incredibly spellbound, a feeling she had not experienced before.

Yamaguchi saw Lilly's concern and gently led her to a beautiful room specifically used for the sacred Tea Ceremony. She was still spellbound and somewhat speechless. The Priest explained the entire cultural activity they were about to undertake; to avoid Lilly feeling she might do something out of time or place.

In a wonderful, deep, yet soft as velvet voice, Yamaguchi told Lilly that the Japanese Tea Ceremony was also known as 'chanoyu' or 'Sado', adding that it was an activity involving the ceremonial preparation and presentation of 'matcha', which is powdered green tea. He said that the event always followed the same pattern and was choreographed, encompassing aesthetics, concerned with the natural appreciation of beauty; Zen philosophy, an intuitive understanding achieved through meditation to attain enlightenment or awakening; and a spiritual connection between the host and guests. The ceremony emphasised mindfulness, respect, purity, and tranquillity, with each moment considered unique and precious.

Lilly turned her beautiful, almond-shaped, liquid brown eyes towards Yamaguchi. Words failed her, but the Priest knew that she was ready to take part in the beautiful ritual of the Japanese Tea Ceremony.

Lilly followed the Priest, noting the somewhat hypnotic aroma of incense. She knelt on a beautifully embroidered red silk cushion he had pointed out to her. Yamaguchi then proceeded to wash the delicate porcelain cups and prepare the powdered green tea. Before handing her the tea, Yamaguchi and Lilly both washed their hands in the most delicate bowls of perfumed water. The most wonderful aroma filled the little room.

Holding the cup with both hands, as was the Japanese custom, the Priest bowed his head and handed Lilly one of the tiny, ever so beautiful cups, so delicate that the light shone through it. The Priest suggested that Lilly Moon Flower remain silent for a little while and take in the occasion, allowing her feelings to take over her mind and body. Lilly could tell that Chief Priest Yamaguchi was totally focused on her and her well-being, ensuring that she had total peace of mind, that their minds were in tandem, leaving her feeling fully relaxed and in unison with Yamaguchi. At that moment, they felt as one, in a time and world entirely of their own.

Without saying another word, Lilly and Yamaguchi sat for some time reflecting on the precious moment they had shared. To Lilly, it felt like an out-of-body experience, deeply moving and utterly enthralling. Yamaguchi then spoke, asking Lilly to tell him about her beautiful name. He was captivated by her grace, tranquility and serenity, qualities he thought were exceptionally rare in someone so young.

Lilly slowly painted a picture of herself, her name, and her two incredibly different yet wonderful families. Yamaguchi could see that this was where Lilly inherited her natural physical beauty and her beautiful soul. The latter moved the Priest to wish to get to know her spiritually. He felt that their minds had joined during the Tea Ceremony, a situation he had tried to achieve on previous occasions. Still, he believed he had never completed the ultimate joining of minds as he had with this exquisite Eurasian girl.

Yamaguchi listened intently to Lilly's explanation of her unusual name, realising that it reflected the union of two strong, thoughtful, and generous-hearted families. To him, she embodied the very best of East and West, a remarkable young woman who, he felt, had been placed on this earth for greatness.

Yamaguchi was left believing that he had been destined to meet this exquisite young woman. He asked if he could be so bold as to tell Lilly a little of his background and how he came to be at the Juganji Temple in Osaka. Lilly replied that she would feel honoured to learn more about him and the tranquil, peaceful temple where her grandfather was eventually laid to rest.

The Priest began his story, explaining that his grandfather, Shinkai Yamaguchi, had heard of the horrors of prisoners in the camps across Japan, learning that many thousands had died during captivity. His grandfather, Shinkai, had researched to establish what had happened to all the prisoners who had been killed in Osaka, wishing to bring peace to those who had perished and, most importantly, their relatives, if he could track them down. Yamaguchi explained that his grandfather, Shinkai, had made it his life's work to create a final resting place for as many Allied Forces who died at the hands of the Japanese military as was humanly possible.

He went on to tell Lilly that Shinkai had contacted the Army Offices of the Allied Forces in 1954, who, together with the Allied War Office, had agreed to release the bodies of more than 1000 men to the Temple, making it their final resting place. Lilly was totally absorbed in what Yamaguchi was saying, feeling overcome with thanks for what Shinkai had done for her family and others who had lost loved ones in Japan.

The Priest told Lilly that, having received the bodies, Shinkai followed the Buddhist custom, which was to cremate the dead and to keep their ashes at the temple before burial for several months. Yamaguchi hesitated for a moment, as if overcome with emotion, before explaining to Lilly that his grandfather had said daily prayers for the lost souls who were in his safekeeping, commenting that he was known to have done this until the day he had died. With a prayer for world peace, Yamaguchi took over the ceremony by reciting daily prayers for the souls being looked after in the Temple, promising he would also now do so until he too passed from this life into his afterlife, where he knew he would join his revered grandfather.

Lilly was not herself at that moment in time; it was as if she had been one with Yamaguchi, the Buddhist Priest from the Juganji Temple. More than that, she felt her grandfather's presence in this holy and tranquil place.

Lilly took her leave with much reluctance. Lilly Moon Flower asked if she would be permitted to revisit the Temple soon, once she had assimilated what she had seen and heard on this most memorable of days. The Priest told Lilly that she was welcome at any time, and indeed, if during her year in Japan she felt she had the time to spare, she could perhaps join a small group of multicultural students on a short retreat. Lilly asked herself, "How much better could this incredible day get?"

Seeing that she was reluctant to make an immediate decision, Yamaguchi promised that if she would permit him to know her address, he would keep her informed of the forthcoming retreat programme so she could think about what it would mean and whether it was something she thought she was strong enough to do and would benefit from.

Lilly left the temple feeling she had met one of the kindest and most sincere people she had ever known, and she was certain she would return one day. Before making such a significant decision, however, she knew she needed time to reflect on what joining a retreat would mean for her, both spiritually and mentally.

Most importantly, Lilly knew she must understand the level of commitment joining a retreat would demand of her.

CHAPTER THIRTY-NINE

During a short break from her studies, and feeling that she was on the verge of making decisions for her future that could impact every member of her family, Lilly took a flight back to the UK to see her parents and grandmother. Intending to stay at her grandmother's cottage in Wales, Orchid and Karl, Lilly's parents, joined them in Wales. Orchid and Karl, along with their son Karl Jun, were all working at Karl's law firm, which gave Lilly the opportunity to catch up with her parents and brother at the same time. Frequent and lengthy phone calls took place between Wales and Shanghai, as Lilly's Chinese grandparents were eager to hear how their beautiful granddaughter was faring.

Lilly talked at length about the opportunity to join a retreat in Osaka at the Temple where her grandfather was buried. Even though she knew she had already made the decision to attend, as she saw this as a potentially life-changing decision, she felt it was only right that she share her thoughts with her family. They listened without comment at first, and when they saw the warmth in her eyes as she spoke about the impact that visiting the Temple and meeting Yamaguchi had had on her, they offered their full support. They understood that the chance for deep meditation was something truly valuable, especially at Lilly's young age.

CHAPTER FORTY

Her brief visit to the UK passed quickly, but Lilly knew she had achieved all she had hoped and felt ready to return to her studies in Osaka. Spending time once again with family seemed to have rejuvenated her, giving her a keen sense of direction. During the following week, Lilly found herself very busy catching up on her course reading material. It was a relief to know that she was slowly feeling part of the University scene and the culture that surrounded student life in Japan.

Family ties were powerful in Japan. This was not at all surprising to Lilly, as growing up with two very close, extended families, each with its own unique norms and culture, gave her a natural affinity to the way in which her Japanese friends frequently spoke of their families and were eager to share their parents with someone so appreciative and tactfully understanding.

One friend, Aiko, meaning "beloved child," who lived with her parents in Osaka near the university, asked Lilly if she would like to join her and her family at a forthcoming festival. The upcoming celebration was called 'The Golden Week' and was one of the biggest celebrations in Japan.

Lilly was intrigued and delighted as each visit seemed to help her assimilate more of the intriguing Japanese culture. Aiko told her that Golden Week, as its name alluded to, was one of the biggest weeks in Japan. She explained that it was, in fact, a series of four national holidays at the end of April and the beginning of May, creating a period of consecutive days off where families could more easily get together and celebrate.

She added that because it was a full week of celebration, families also treated it as a time for rest, and it was one of the most anticipated holidays of the year. Lilly felt privileged to be invited to join Aiko's family, knowing that it would involve visiting various relatives and taking part in a range of cultural events.

Lilly and Aiko were sitting together in Aiko's parents' beautiful Japanese villa, so richly decorated with vibrant colours, the day felt like a wonderful holiday before the festivities began. She learnt that many Japanese people used this time to travel domestically or even internationally, visiting family. The atmosphere in the villa was jubilant, richly decorated with lanterns and featuring some of the most magnificent flowers Lilly had ever seen.

As the week progressed, the two friends toured several Japanese towns, each hosting different festivals that featured traditional music, parades, and food stalls serving the most exquisite Japanese street food Lilly had ever tasted. When initially planning her visit to Japan, Lilly had no idea of the richness of family life that she would be privileged to share. Being there for a string of significant festivals, Golden Week provided Lilly with the chance to experience Japan's rich cultural heritage, from traditional activities to modern festivals. She felt incredibly lucky and humbled by how Aiko's family had taken her into their home and included her in their personal family festivities.

CHAPTER FORTY-ONE

Lilly found that her studies and life in general were moving fast. She had sent a series of postcards to her family. With so much to share, she found it easier to write and post letters, knowing they would mean so much to her family, who had no way of experiencing the wonders that Japan had to offer at the present time.

When not studying or actively engaged at the University, Lilly's thoughts frequently focused on Yamaguchi, the kind Buddhist Priest she had met at the Juganji Temple. What really played on her mind was the invitation to join a retreat. She was unsure of the expectations of her and what format the retreat would take. Following her visit, Yamaguchi had, as promised, sent her an outline programme for the forthcoming event.

The contents eased some of Lilly's concerns, but she knew that her personal connection to the Temple, with her grandfather buried there, might not be known to others and could influence how they perceived her interest. Even so, she took the important step of returning to see Yamaguchi to tell him that she would love to be part of the upcoming retreat.

Pleased that Lilly had decided to join, Yamaguchi explained that there would be periods of meditation, talks on aspects of Buddhism, as well as Buddhist rituals. However, the retreat welcomed participants from many different religions and cultures, and there would be an opportunity for Lilly to speak to learned people from many faiths and backgrounds. Yamaguchi emphasised that, while it was not a Silent Retreat, there would be many meditation sessions and more extended periods of silence to allow for reflection. Lilly decided that she would indeed join the Retreat.

With a mix of excitement and trepidation, Lilly travelled to join the retreat. As part of introducing themselves, participants provided a synopsis of their lives and experiences thus far. Lilly was pleased to see there was a mix of different nationalities, ages, and cultural backgrounds on the retreat.

Yamaguchi introduced himself to the group by stating that he was there to offer them the opportunity for reflection and meditation, adding that it was a chance to spend time away from their usual daily activities in a "spiritual or contemplative" environment. He commented on the pressures of modern-day life and the conflicting demands that going on a retreat enabled them to step back from and regain a sense of calm and perspective. He told them that during the time they spent together, they would go through a process aimed at quietening their minds and removing distractions.

Lilly felt strange for a day or so. Even though outgoing in many ways, she was still in turmoil following her visit to her grandfather's grave and her time spent meditating on her own with Yamaguchi. She approached it much like she had when settling into university life, by actively engaging with other participants and hearing about their experiences, travels, and hopes for the future.

Lilly felt a deep sense of peace and tranquillity in the presence of the Chief Priest, Yamaguchi. He was able to guide participants effortlessly into a flow state, a feeling of harmony between mind and body, where they became completely absorbed and intensely focused on him. Nothing else mattered at that moment in time. Lilly wondered whether she would ever be able to leave this truly tranquil environment in which she had unexpectedly but willingly tumbled. She felt calm and transformed.

As the retreat came to an end, Lilly knew she would have to leave this beautiful place where she had found such peace of mind and thoughtfulness. Lilly was aware that she had changed; the impact that Yamaguchi had on her was something she could not quite understand. "Just where do I go from here?" she thought. However, Lilly was already talking to Yamaguchi about a plan for the future.

On departure, the participants went their separate ways, knowing that they had formed friendships and connections that they believed would last a lifetime, having shared something truly special.

Lilly believed that she had truly changed as a person, and as her studies in Osaka were coming to an end, she felt it was time to head back to the UK and begin her plans for her very exciting and, what promised to be, an extremely challenging future.

CHAPTER FORTY-TWO

The homecoming was incredibly special for Lilly. Her parents and grandparents met up in the UK for the reunion; all felt that this was something very special. And they were right, as it was something that would impact all of their lives, but in different ways.

Everyone was delighted with the way Lilly had settled into Japanese culture. From her postcards and letters, they could see how much she had grown and how level-headed she was becoming as a person.

Constance was mesmerised by the change in Lilly. Knowing she was born to be something extraordinary, she felt that the closeness between herself and her grandchild had morphed into something neither could fully understand.

The beautiful woman they met at the airport was no longer the lovely young girl they had sent off on her journey to Japan. Lilly was somehow so very different. They all agreed that Lilly had matured, yet she had lost none of her natural loveliness. There was a new glow about her, an inner warmth and magnificence that they could not quite explain. It was as if Lilly had discovered her north, her direction in life. She radiated happiness.

Whilst the postcards and letters had provided both families with an overview of where Lilly was and what she was doing, they had no idea of the bombshell she was about to lay before them.

Lilly spoke at length about her learning while at the University of Osaka, having achieved a distinction in the studies she had focused on, which she knew would be included in her final degree when returning to Belfast University for the concluding semester.

She spoke about the time she spent at the grave of her grandfather, and naturally, Constance was eager to see the photograph that she had taken. She held it in her hand while her granddaughter told them more and more about her incredible trip and findings. The way Lilly spoke about Yamaguchi suggested that he had had a huge influence on her. She described in detail how he seemed to understand her to a depth she had not previously experienced.

Having acclimatised following her long journey from Osaka and the deep feelings and thoughts that had accompanied her time spent on her retreat, Lilly felt she was now ready to share her feelings, ideas, and plans with her family, knowing that to achieve them, she would surely need their help and support. She firmly believed that the red ribbon that bound them all together would support the exciting future she faced.

She started by explaining that as part of her studies at the University of Osaka, she had been both intrigued and enlightened by the issues faced by thousands of orphaned children in Japan. She went on to say that this had initially come as a surprise, but upon reflection on her studies, the reasons were relatively easy to understand, although challenging to solve. In a country with falling birth rates coupled with an ageing population, Japan was facing an alarming demographic crisis, with thousands of children slipping through the cracks.

Lilly explained that Japan's foster care system seemed to have created a bubble of isolation from society, through which children were leaving ill-equipped for the transition into adulthood. She described how children were moved from abusive homes to institutions, often facing poor living conditions, physical abuse, and very little support or planning for their futures.

With a smile on her face and a sense of certainty and peace, Lilly told her captivated family that she intended to return to Japan and work with Chief Priest Yamaguchi. She explained the profound impact her visit and time spent on the Retreat had had on her. She now knew what she wanted to do with her life: to work with Yamaguchi to establish a charity focusing on children leaving the care system. Their aim was to provide financial support and social assistance during the critical transition into higher education, whether in Japan or abroad.

Constance was particularly keen to hear more about the plight of the orphaned children. She had, for many years, wished to help children in the Far East if the opportunity arose. Constance thought of the joy she would derive from supporting her granddaughter and Chief Priest Yamaguchi with their charity.

Lilly Moon Flower spoke at length about her initial research, which showed that children separated from family-based institutions faced serious challenges in everyday life. Unless they received individualised, focused care, they were often deprived of basic necessities and experiences, leaving them disconnected from their peers and society. Her research also highlighted that even after children transitioned out of care, these disadvantages frequently persisted, causing them to fall outside formal learning opportunities entirely.

Lilly explained that, in discussions with Yamaguchi, he had shared his long-held desire to reduce the isolation experienced by young people leaving foster care, which was blighting their life chances. He told her that less than 15% of children coming out of care completed further education. Even those who managed the transition into higher education often felt isolated from their peers.

This formed the foundation of the school support scheme they wished to establish, situated within the tranquil grounds of the Juganji Buddhist Temple. They saw their role as guides for children leaving care without relatives or contacts, providing support, guidance, and financial assistance through bursaries.

Lilly's plan for the future occupied much of her grandmother's thoughts over the following three months. Lilly arranged a three-way telephone conversation between herself, her grandmother, and Yamaguchi, who had sought legal advice on setting up the charity, to be called **'Joy and Hope'**. Lilly was to fly back to Japan within the next six months, following completion of her degree at Belfast University and after settling matters at home, as she was uncertain when or if she would return permanently to the UK or Shanghai.

In the meantime, Constance liaised with Karl, her son-in-law, who had law practices in Belfast and Shanghai. Karl had agreed to handle Constance's affairs, being within reasonable reach of both Wales and Osaka. The decision was made that Constance would set up a Charitable Incorporated Organisation (CIO) and appoint the two named trustees: Lilly Moon Flower and Yamaguchi.

CHAPTER FORTY-THREE

Constance felt elated that she had found a truly worthy cause to support, feeling blessed to have achieved this during her lifetime, which had always been her wish. She felt at peace knowing that she had achieved so much during her lifetime.

She knew that her experiences and travels around the world had enriched her both mentally and physically. Constance had stayed in close contact with her relatives around the world, and they all knew that she wished to bring together elements of East and West as she departed from her earthly life. Constance was aware that her daughter, Orchid, and her husband, Karl, had expressed their wish to play a key role in planning for her departure to her welcomed afterlife.

Constance frequently found herself reflecting on aspects of her life that had impacted her, and two always came to mind. One was the courage she knew she had shown when escaping Hong Kong with her two young children. Her strength, her dragon, knew no bounds at that time, as it had meant leaving her husband behind.

The second profound impact came from her chance meeting with the mighty, wonderful Sea Lord, Shangdi. She had held onto the belief that they would surely meet again somehow. Constance occasionally felt that Shangdi was attempting to contact her. The Hungry Ghost Festival was particularly notable; Constance was sure he had tried to reach out to her at that time. On one of her trips back to the Far East, she had witnessed the same, and yet, how could that be?

Life was becoming slower for Constance. She knew she was no longer able to do the things she once managed with ease, especially travelling to visit her family and friends.

During a tranquil week, Constance received a most unusual gift by mail. The box it came in was strange in so many ways. She looked at it and lifted the package, realising that it held fluid. Gingerly opening the package, Constance found an odd-looking plant with the most disgusting-looking branch growing out of the side of the otherwise plush green leaves. The plant had been cushioned in cotton wool and other materials to protect and maintain it during its travels. No note was inside the package, and nothing indicated what the plant was or who it had come from.

Not being sure of the best way to maintain the health of the strange-looking plant, Constance thought it best to keep it in the package it had arrived in, giving her time to research how to care for it. She rested the package in her bedroom, overlooking the beautiful Welsh hillside.

CHAPTER FORTY-FOUR

Constance died with her family around her. She held the beautiful, cool green jade stone in her hand. Her relatives were aware of her wish to include some Eastern traditions in her funeral.

They had arranged for a fantastic, red tissue papercraft replica of the mighty, majestic Chinese Junk, the Shangdu, to be made for her.

Those surrounding her bed as Constance passed watched in disbelief as she gently reached up her hand. With a beautiful smile on her face, which seemed to have taken on a soft glow, she took hold of the silky red ribbon the mighty, majestic Sea Lord Shangdi held out to her. Those gathered around her bed watched in disbelief at what they were witnessing, as Constance and Shangdi sailed away together on the magnificent, smooth turquoise seas, their spirits carried beyond the physical world on the majestic Chinese Junk, the Shangdu.

At the same time, those surrounding her became aware of a lovely, heady, alluring fragrance. Looking around, they saw to their amazement that the previously green-leafed, somewhat ugly plant sitting close to Constance had bloomed, opening up with just one absolutely magnificent, alluring Moon Flower. People looked at each other in disbelief, realising that the Moon Flower had opened during the last night of Constance's life, transforming the odd-looking flower into something of such beauty that it took their breath away.

The Chinese red thread brought them together, as this was their destiny. The whimsical red ribbon may tangle, but it will never break. Their Dragons were seen to join hands and follow them into eternity. At the same time, the lovely Moon Flower closed its beautiful, aromatic petals, gently rested its head, and died.

The End

AUTHOR BIO

Irene Turnbull-Banham has lived a life shaped by love, loss and a deep curiosity about people and their stories. The widow of an Army Officer who passed away in 2012, she spent many years between Northern Ireland and the Far East. These experiences strengthened her appreciation of courage, culture and quiet resilience.

Her career with a global bank took her across the Pacific Rim, where she absorbed the histories and traditions that influence her writing. However, it was her own family's past, including her mother-in-law's escape from Hong Kong with her children and her father-in-law's endurance in a Japanese POW camp, that inspired this novel.

Irene believes that we each carry an inner strength that rises when life demands it. She now lives in North Wales with her husband, John, and their much-loved Sharpie puppies, Chen-Chen and Pang-Pang, and continues to write stories that honour ordinary people in extraordinary times.

ACKNOWLEDGEMENT

I want to give my heartfelt thanks to my husband, John, for his help and support during what has, at times, been an enjoyable, somewhat emotional journey. My thanks also go to my daughters, who have shown such enthusiasm for encouraging me to complete the book I have carried in my head and in a box of Second World War memorabilia for some fourteen years. I would also like to thank my son-in-law, Phil Green, for his inspirational help in creating a wonderful cover for the book.